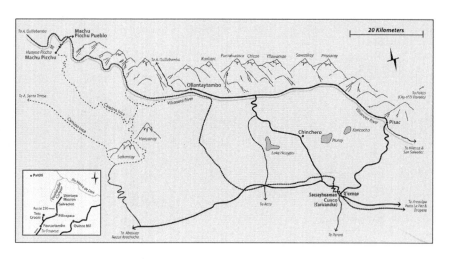

# THE SACRED VALLEY OF THE INCAS

# TANIS AND THE MAGICAL VALLEY
## A Journey through the Inca Heartland

*Written by Sixto Paz Wells*

*Illustrated by*

*Tanis Paz Torres and Marina Torres Puglianini*

*Translated from the Spanish by Laurie Friedler*

*Edited by Maureen Gaffney*

ISBN 978-1-300-71252-7

# Table of Contents

"First we learn to hear, and then we learn to look... much later and perhaps after middle age... we learn to listen and after we listen it is possible to see.

When we see, we fall in love with life and with that love we become wise, because with love, intelligence and knowledge becomes wisdom. As you begin to know wisdom, you seem cold and distant to some and yet the heart burns with a compassion that is difficult to hide. In either case, all is well..."

— *Pepe Cabot Gibert*

# Author's Introduction

This book came about as a result of numerous requests from young people and adults alike to write about UFOs and extraterrestrials. It is a sequel to *Tanis y la Esfera Dorada* (*Tanis and the Golden Sphere*), my first book for young people. While continuing its predecessor's themes, *Tanis y el Mágico Cuzco* (*Tanis and the Magical Cuzco*) complements them with information about the ancient wisdom of the Andean people who had regular contact with extraterrestrials.

Although fictional, *Tanis y el Mágico Cuzco* was informed by my personal experiences and those of my wife and daughters. Certain parts were inspired by the experiences of others—especially children who over the years had shared their stories with me, trusting perhaps that I would value those stories and help them understand them.

The young people now being born on Earth are old souls. Many are star children who have come to fulfill a mission that we must support as we fulfill our own. However, we cannot help these children who represent the future of humanity if we ourselves do not change and learn to listen.

As they did for the first one, my daughter Tanis and my wife Marina made the book's drawings. And everyone who contributed to *Tanis y el Mágico Cuzco* believes that by making its stories known and by sharing them, we are putting together a huge jigsaw puzzle.

I could never have imagined the variety of anecdotes *Tanis y la Esfera Dorada* would elicit nor the warm reception it would get from all over the world. I hope *Tanis y el Mágico Cuzco* is similarly received and, beyond providing entertainment, serves as a guide to light-seekers out there.

***Sixto Paz Wells*** — Lima, Peru

# Translator's Introduction

*Tanis and the Magical Valley: A Journey through the Inca Heartland* narrates the wisdom and wonders a girl named Tanis experiences as she travels with her family in the Andean highlands. Its events are fictionalized real-life experiences based on two short novels by Sixto Paz Wells.

Sixto has had direct contact with extraterrestrials since 1974 and travels widely to speak about UFOs, ETs, and the evolution of consciousness, but his main message is about the transformative power of love. Sixto also leads groups to sacred places in South America, Mesoamerica, the Caribbean, Africa, Europe, the Middle East, and the Far East. Although he has written eighteen books, until now only *The Invitation* has been published in English.

In 2010 Sixto and I jointly led a pilgrimage to sites in Cuzco and Peru's Sacred Valley on which we explored Andean cosmology as well as methods for harmonizing our own bioenergies. On the last day of our trip, someone asked which of his many books Sixto would like to see translated into English next. Surprising everyone, he said *Tanis y el Mágico Cuzco*. When I asked why, he said, "It's about the journey we just completed."

Since I love the book's subject matter and greatly respect Sixto and his work, I translated it along with related RAMA documents outlining practices for awakening consciousness and developing the master teacher within. I posted those documents on www.RahmaUnitedStates.com as a way of giving back—what Andean people call ayni.

The Spanish version of *Tanis and the Magical Valley* was written for an audience familiar with Peru's history and geography, so it had to be adapted for American readers. Maureen Gaffney and I added information about Peru as well as a prologue with excerpts from *Tanis y la Esfera Dorada* for essential background. We also broke the chapters into segments that follow the trip's itinerary, added a map, and developed a glossary.

Now after two years, *Tanis and the Magical Valley: A Journey Through the Inca Heartland* has emerged to honor the meeting of condor and eagle—a prophesied coming together of spiritual traditions from South America (the condor) and North America (the eagle). I will be forever grateful to Sixto for the opportunity to share the book's far-reaching themes with a general, English language readership. I hope those readers find it valuable.

*Laurie Friedler* — Madison CT, 2012

# 1

# *Prologue: Nocturnal Journeys*

It all began simply enough. One night when I was five and a half, an odd light woke me from sleep. I opened my eyes to find my bedroom flooded with an eerie blue glow. I'd never seen anything like it and didn't know where it was coming from.

I went to the window to see if something outside was lighting up the room, but everything looked normal. The garden below was as dark as usual at night. And the sky was full of stars. As I gazed up, a bright star bigger than the rest caught my eye.

I always wish on shooting stars even though Father says they aren't stars. He says they're meteors—burning fragments from other worlds. But there were no shooting stars then so I focused on the big, bright star and made a wish.

As soon as I did, the star got brighter and began to turn and twist. Its movement bothered me so I returned to bed and pulled the covers over my head.

I was just dozing off when something landed on the bed with a plop. Thinking it was my cat Chuchi, I turned on a light to pull him under the covers. When I saw that he wasn't there I got spooked and ran to my sister's room to slip in bed with her. Yearim's her name but I call her Yaya. She's such a heavy sleeper she never stirred and I awoke with her hair in my face.

During breakfast I told my parents and Yaya about the light and the weight on my bed. Mother asked why hadn't I gone to her and Father's room. Yaya suggested I might have confused the star with a planet, which would be bigger and brighter than a star.

"It wasn't a planet," I said emphatically. "It turned and twisted. Planets don't do that!"

"Then it was probably an airplane," Yaya replied.

I was getting irritated. Yaya is two years older than me but sometimes she acts like a know-it-all. "No!" I insisted, "It was not an airplane!"

Father intervened, saying, "When someone sees an object in the sky they can't classify, the object is called an unidentified flying object—UFO for short. UFOs can be any number of rationally explainable things, starting with broken parts from rockets or earth-orbiting satellites. They can also be meteorites and atmospheric phenomena like mirages or reflections in the clouds from city lights. But some UFOs, like secret military weapons or spaceships from other worlds, are inexplicable."

"How can I tell if a UFO is a spaceship?" I asked.

"That's not easy," he said, "unless you have a close sighting. Then the object must behave in a way that differs from all other possibilities—and it must behave intelligently."

I understood the part about intelligent behavior. And the idea of other worlds intrigued me. "Are there other planets like Earth?" I asked.

"There are many worlds, Tanis," replied Father, "more than grains of sand in the sea."

"Is there life on those other worlds?" Yaya asked, suddenly interested in the topic.

"There must be, and one day we shall find out," he answered. "Science has established that the beginnings of life go back to organic molecules that float in the cosmic dust between galaxies. Just as wind carries seeds from one island to another, it's possible for meteors to pick up cosmic dust from outer space and take it into a planet's atmosphere, bringing life."

I still wasn't clear what the light and the star were about but I knew one thing for sure: what had happened the night before deeply altered my sense of the world.

When Mother was putting me to bed that night, I asked what to do if the light came back. She placed my palms together in prayer position and, holding them between her hands, we prayed to my guardian angel for protection. Mother assured me that nothing bad was going to happen. "If the light appears again," she said, kissing me goodnight, "it will be a good light."

The light did not appear that night. However I dreamt that human looking light beings were calling me, asking me to accompany them somewhere. They took me to a colorful, light-filled place where children were learning in outdoor classrooms.

For nearly a month the light did not return. Then one night a loud drone awakened me. It sounded like a giant beehive buzzing in my bedroom. I bolted up and saw a sphere of light the size of a volleyball hovering behind my window curtain.

My nose began itching so I turned to get a tissue. When I turned around again the sphere was right in front of me. I opened my mouth to scream but no sound came out and the sphere zoomed through the window as if it had no glass.

Filled with a mix of fear and excitement, my heart was racing. When it slowed to a more regular rhythm, I lay back and considered my situation. I was okay but it was the middle of a school night. So I covered my face with my comfort blanket, leaving a peephole to see the window, and went back to sleep.

Next day I didn't say anything about the sphere. Father never raised the possibility that the twisting star could be an extraterrestrial. Now I thought it might be. And if last night's visitor was an ET, I was curious to learn more about it.

I tried to stay awake that night just in case the sphere returned. But I was deep in a dream world when a bright light woke me up. In a flash, my heart began racing. The sphere entered through my window and hovered in midair a short distance from my bed. Mostly red with an occasional flash of yellow or bright blue, it began to inspect my room. It quickly scanned the furniture and hovered over the hamster's cage. Then it left.

Somewhat disappointed, I went back to sleep and dreamt of being transported to a place with blue-domed buildings. In many ways the dream seemed like a continuation of other dreams. Children were playing with spheres that resembled my nighttime visitor. Some were clear. Others were colored. One seemed big enough to hold my father. I was just thinking that when a tall person emerged from it and walked down a garden path. Flowers near the path practically danced and colored butterflies flitted among them. The last thing I recall was the gentle sound of music.

At breakfast next morning, I shared that dream with my parents. They were delighted to hear it, perhaps because it was only a dream and a pleasant one at that.

Later on, when Yaya and I were in the car with Father, I asked if there were such things as small UFOs—UFOs the size of a volleyball.

Father studied me for a moment before saying, "I've read of spheres that size in a book. Air force pilots reported seeing spheres of light spying on their airplanes during World War II. Some said they passed right through the plane's fuselage. Assuming the spheres were secret weapons, certain pilots called them foo-fighters and the name stuck."

"What's a foo-fighter?" I inquired.

"The spheres resembled fireballs and the French word for fire is pronounced something like foo so Americans spelled it f-o-o. There's no evidence that they were weapons. They could have been remote-controlled robotic cameras."

"Maybe the spheres were afraid we'd attack them," I suggested.

"They probably weren't afraid," he replied. "They were probably trying not to start any trouble. If foo-fighters were to appear openly, they might cause a world crisis by challenging conventional ideas of what's possible. Certain countries might feel threatened and react aggressively, bringing great harm to many people."

"If it was up to me," Yaya said hotly, "I'd fight the bad people and help the good ones by imposing peace and ending sickness and poverty."

Father responded with a wisdom teaching I still recall word for word: "In the spiritual path as well as in life itself, one must learn to discern between what one can do, what one wants to do, and what one needs to do." He went on to explain that those who fail to make such distinctions cause more harm than good. Help that's imposed only invites rebellion or rejection. It's better to let others mature and gain consciousness in their own way. So the best help foo-fighters or UFOs can offer us is to not interfere with our growth process.

In some ways that was how my parents were treating me. Though unsure that my reports about the light and the sphere were true, they were trying to find out what was going on. They were also letting me work things out, as best I could, on my own.

A few nights later, the sphere showed up again. As it passed through my window, it made a sound like branches rustling in the wind. This time the sphere was gold and bigger than before. My feelings got hurt when it went directly to the door of my room without stopping at my bed. Still, I followed it into Yaya's room, where it scared Chuchi. Then I trailed it to my parents' room where it inspected the photos on Mother's dresser.

That's when I noticed the sphere's big eye. Now that I had a good look, the eye was its most distinct feature. It was also something I could relate to, so I decided Ojito was a good name for it. Ojo means eye, but I added a friendly –ito. I felt it would be rude to simply call the sphere Ojo.

Ojito left after scanning Mother's photos. When he returned a few nights later, he explored other areas of the house and I followed him to the den. He seemed curious about the family photos, so I pulled out our albums and showed them to him one by one. When I held up a photo of myself, he almost bounced up and down when he recognized me.

Encouraged by this, I pulled out a book and showed him pictures of different countries. I showed him a photo of Earth taken from outer space and the different types of people and animals on the planet. Then I went back to the photo of Earth and pointed to it and then to myself to indicate that's where I lived. When I asked where he came from, he moved to the bookshelf and made a book slide out. I laughed as it floated in midair.

The book hovered over my lap and landed very gently there. Then the pages flipped at great speed, stopping at a photo of what looked like a planet. I asked Ojito if that's where he came from and his response was a rapid up and down movement, as if nodding yes. I looked at the caption and sounded out the syllables of Ganymede.

I observed him for a moment, wondering if he came alone or in the company of others. I had a sense that he wasn't alone.

"Have you come to explore," I asked, "or are you looking for someone?" First he moved sideways and then up and down. I guessed that meant no to the first question and yes to the second. Communicating without words was tricky, so I thought maybe it would be better if I tried one question at a time. With that in mind, I asked, "Who are you looking for?"

Ojito pulled out a photo of me and floated it into my hands. Suddenly overcome by a great heaviness, I began yawning, excused myself, and went to lie on the couch.

I was surprised when I woke the next morning in my own bed. I assumed the stuff with the photos had been a dream until I overheard Mother complaining that Father had left a mess in the den. Books had been removed from the shelves and scattered, along with family photos, all over the room. When he protested that he had not removed any books or left a mess of any kind, I knew it had really happened.

Later I told Mother. She looked doubtful and asked if I had imagined it. I said no and, taking responsibility for the mess in the den, I apologized. Looking baffled, Mother went to talk with Father. That night Father had a bedtime chat with me.

"Tanis, you know I love you very much, but even love has a limit," he warned. "It's not amusing for you to be fantasizing and imagining things that involve others and make extra work for them. There is a moment for everything, but if you don't accept reality you will suffer much in life."

"I had to tell Mother about the mess," I replied, now on the verge of tears. "I had no idea she wouldn't believe me. I'm telling the truth, Father. I'm not imagining the sphere."

"Okay, Tanis," he said, pulling me close. "Start again from the beginning."

So I told him everything, just the way it happened. He didn't say he believed me, but he said if the sphere returned I should wake him so he could see for himself. I agreed and, mindful of his request, went to sleep that night hoping Ojito would appear. But he didn't.

Nothing happened for the next few nights. Then one night after Father read my bedtime story something did happen.

It was past midnight when Mother climbed the spiral staircase to the roof deck above our house. She was bringing hot tea for Father and herself as they prepared to spend the cool night outside. I didn't know it, but my parents were keeping a vigil.

Shortly after 1:30 a.m. they saw a strange light in the sky. Seconds later, all the lights in the neighborhood went out. In the darkness they saw a bright light expand in midair into a banana-like shape from which many luminous, colored spheres emerged. Each sphere drifted to a different house. A golden sphere of about a foot in diameter entered my bedroom window.

Ojito was already in my room when I woke up. He surprised me by saying, "Hola, Tanis!" It was the first time he'd used my name and the first time he had spoken. And he spoke Spanish in an easygoing man's voice. The oddest thing was *how* I heard him: I felt and heard his voice inside my head but it made no sound in the room.

He said I should stay in bed and relax because he wanted me to try journeying. He directed me to inhale deeply, hold my breath for a while, and exhale through my nose. Continuing to do that, he assured me, would help me stay alert and remember what happened.

I did as he suggested. He asked me to imagine I was lying on a sandy beach as gentle waves washed over my feet and legs. He said each time the waves ebbed they would draw uneasiness away from my body and allow me to sink deeper into the sand.

I imagined waves washing over my body again and again, gradually going higher—to my hips, my shoulders, then my head, until I felt the sea holding me up as I floated. After a while I seemed to be floating in the air next to him. The sensation was quite pleasant and reminded me of how I move in dreams.

"You just began an astral journey," he informed me. "You will temporarily leave your physical body and travel with me in your astral body."

I was trying to imagine what an astral body was…

"An astral body is a vehicle for your emotions and aspirations," Ojito explained before I asked. "It's a spirit body, a double of your physical body that travels and has experiences as you dream."

He moved to the window. I felt myself moving with him and turned to see my body lying on the bed. Then I got scared because I looked dead.

"You're not dead, Tanis—and you're not about to die," Ojito assured me. "But an astral journey is like a death because you stop being the person you think you are and become the person you have always been."

"Can you read my mind?"

"Yes," he replied. "I can understand your feelings and thoughts directly, without words."

What would it mean, I thought, to become the person I've always been?

"Bit by bit, Tanis, you will learn that your personality is only part of who you are," Ojito said. "As for the question of who you've always been—who you really are, you will realize that soon enough. You need to look inside."

I wondered how I could look inside.

"With the eyes of the heart, dear child."

Like the neighborhood, the whole house was dark. Using Father's small book light to guide them, my parents made their way to my room as quickly as they could. They found me on my bed in a deep, trance-like sleep, so Mother covered me with blankets.

At this point my parents' night watch had confirmed some of what I told them. It also indicated that ours was not the only house being visited by a luminous sphere. But the night was not over, so they settled into a corner of my room to continue their vigil.

Though she tried to stay awake, Mother eventually fell asleep. Father read with his book light until 5:30 when the light seemed to be losing power.

He was about to get new batteries when a bright blue light filled the room, waking Mother. Then a golden sphere entered the room, moved toward my bed, and hovered a few feet above where I lay.

My parents stared in astonishment as a translucent double of me emerged from the golden sphere and, floating gently down, dropped into my body. Mother recalls that at the precise moment when the two bodies—my astral and physical bodies—reunited I let out sigh and, still sleeping, rolled onto my side.

Mother and Father watched as the sphere approached them. In a state of wonder, Father reached out to touch it but the sphere recoiled from a contact shock and zoomed so forcefully through the window that the window frame vibrated. A short time later, the house lights came on.

After making sure I was okay, Father went to sleep in his own bed while Mother slept on the floor beside mine. Both were in the room when I awoke next morning. They sat on my bed and asked what had happened during the night. I said I felt tired. It seemed I'd done so many things in my dreams…

# 2

## *My Birthday Trip*

A few days before my eighth birthday, Mother returned from the year-end meeting at my school. She briefly explained what the teacher said about my scholastic performance and the schedule for the coming year. Then she went into great detail about what happened after the meeting.

Once official business was done, a number of women stayed to chat about their children and some worrisome behaviors. One mother had been surprised when her son said he came from the stars. She laughed and tried to change the subject but her son grew serious and insisted that, even though she was his mother now, he had been her father before. The woman got upset when the boy pretended to be her father. What unsettled her most, however, was that in his role-playing he had mannerisms and viewpoints just like those of her father who died before the boy was born.

Another woman was worried about her youngest daughter. "She stays up at night staring at the stars in the sky, saying she misses her home—even crying sometimes," the woman said. "I explain that her home is here but she keeps insisting that she came from the stars. I've taken her to a psychologist and hope it's just a phase."

A third woman's son sometimes saw himself with a different face, commanding a spaceship in a large intergalactic fleet. "It must be something he saw on television," said the woman. "Children are so sensitive to what they hear and watch. My priest advised me to keep a close eye on him and forbid him to watch science fiction shows."

A young mother said she didn't think TV was so bad. "It keeps my children quiet and helps me find a little time for myself. As soon as my kids finish their homework, I let them watch TV and play video games or use the computer. When they start in with their fairytales, I don't pay any attention—they often get overly imaginative. For example, my son insists that he sees a man in white inside our house, but no one else in the family does. I don't know," she said with a nervous laugh, "maybe it's a ghost."

When someone mentioned a new drug for hyperactivity that had few side effects, Mother spoke up: "Children need to be children—to run, jump, and be active. I know it's easier if they're quiet, but let's not fault them for being kids. We should spend time with them, doing creative projects or outdoor activities. Medicating children just to keep them quiet can have bad long-term effects on their health. And why discourage them from sharing their experiences?"

Mother sighed and then said, "My husband and I want our girls to be able to talk to us about anything. For several years now my younger daughter has been saying she sees a luminous sphere in her room from time to time. She and the sphere communicate telepathically and have developed some kind of friendship. Although it took time for us to accept such an extraordinary idea, my husband and I came to believe it when we saw the sphere for ourselves!"

For a moment there was silence in the room as everyone looked at Mother, then someone changed the subject. Within minutes, most of the women excused themselves. As the group dispersed, a woman came up to my mother and said, "I believe you, Señora. I often see luminous orbs in the night sky—I believe they're UFOs. And I'm sure many of the women who were in this room have also seen them, but they're afraid to say so because they don't want to look foolish or be ridiculed."

That woman left and my teacher asked for a word with Mother. "Señora," she said, "you should be proud of your daughter's accomplishments. She's an outstanding student and you've done an admirable job of supporting her learning process at home."

Then dropping her voice, she said, "We need to discuss something Tanis has been doing. She's been telling classmates about her adventures with a luminous sphere. I told her a good imagination is important but it's also important to distinguish fact from fiction. Tanis said you told her the same thing and yet you confirmed that the sphere was real...

"What has happened," my teacher explained, "is that other children have been saying similar things—even claiming to see spheres. I'm telling you this because not everyone is open minded about such things, and other parents may become concerned. It's a difficult situation. Um…well, I'm sure you understand."

"Of course, I understand," said Mother. "The experiences Tanis has with the sphere have been thoroughly discussed at home. Everyone in my family has experienced it as real."

At that point Mother recalled something she had read. "It's sad that humans so often seem like 'thought of' beings rather than thinkers," she declared. "Our parents have thought us, society has thought us, and we go through life being thought of by others. This leaves little room for us to think for ourselves."

She was silent for a moment—as was my teacher. "Why," Mother continued, "are we afraid to look at things with a truly open mind? If heaven and earth hold more than we can comprehend, why is it hard to believe the experiences our children so innocently share with us?"

Taking my teacher's hands, Mother continued, "I realize such a viewpoint may be too much for some people. So don't worry, I'll talk with Tanis and ask her to have more discretion. She won't raise the topic again at school or with her classmates."

Once she had conveyed all that happened at school, Mother was quiet. She and Father kept their eyes on me during an interval in which no one said anything. Finally I lowered my eyes and told them not to worry. I'd be more discrete in the future.

After dinner, my parents asked what I wanted as a birthday gift. "I wish we could all take a trip to Cuzco and the Sacred Valley during summer vacation," I answered. "I've heard lots about it from you but I'd like to see it for myself—with you and Yaya."

"Yes, let's go!" cried my sister.

"Very well," replied Father as Mother nodded, "I'll look into it!"

In addition to the promised trip, my parents gave me a surprise party on my actual birthday. Some classmates came and we had a wonderful afternoon, playing tag in the park, swinging at a piñata full of candies and trinkets, singing karaoke, and dancing.

I fell asleep that night happily thinking of what a lovely day it had been.

*Ojito and Tanis over Sacsayhuamán*

# 3

## *The Talking Stone*

Ojito and I were somewhere in the mountains at night. The sky was bright with stars, but the ground was dark and I saw little there until his glow illuminated an immense stone wall.

When I wondered where we were, Ojito explained that we were in Cuzco and suggested I examine the wall. I saw a large inclined surface made of finely chiseled stones that seemed very old. Something about the antiquity of the wall stirred deep feelings within me.

"Centuries ago that wall was part of a temple," he informed me. "Touch it and you'll be able to sense its history. Your mind's eye will see the many events it took in, the history it remembers."

Ojito urged me to focus on what I could feel, so I put my hands on the wall. The stones felt cold and hard. Strong and—to my great surprise—also full of life.

"Everything has life, even stones," he noted. "Stones and people are made of the same materials; the human vibration is just faster than that of stones. To understand the history of the stones, you must become acquainted with them. In addition to your hands, put your face and ears to them. Tune in to their vibration. Listen to their whisper."

I did. "Sounds like an engine, maybe a cat's purr," I reported.

Ojito guided me to center my attention on one stone, which I did. After a while I realized she was lamenting that people have forgotten stones have souls. She was sad that no one talked to stones anymore.

"Good," he encouraged. "Now have a conversation."

I wasn't sure how, so I tried using telepathy as Ojito and I do. I concentrated on one question: How does it feel to be in the wall? Before long I sensed an answer.

"I'm part of something important. I serve as a link between stones that, together, create a useful whole. This wall was once part of a great temple dedicated to the sun, the moon, the stars, lightning, and the rainbow, as well as to the invisible and incomprehensible origin of all things. Each stone was held and meditated upon before being placed in the wall. The wall looks different than it did originally, but it is essentially the sanctuary wall the ancient ones envisioned in their hearts and minds and created with their hands."

I wondered what such temples were like.

"The ancient temples were built without doors," the stone informed me. "Their walls had many portals and wide openings to let in the light of God's love, embodied in the rays of the sun. The very structure of the temple reminded people to renew themselves every day by opening up to God's love and letting it flow through them."

"Some of my sister-stones were taken from this wall and used to make walls in churches where stones are just stones, material of no importance that can be put in a structure without deliberation." At that point, the stone communicated what seemed like a sigh.

Ojito urged me to find out if she had a message for me, so I asked.

"Stay open," the stone advised. "The light radiating from the source beyond the sun enters you in a different way each and every day. Do not shut yourself off from it. Let the light enrich you. Let the light accompany you in new ways each moment of your life. You are not the same person today that you were yesterday, nor will you be the same person tomorrow."

I was considering all that when the stone added, "You and I will meet again."

I wanted to know when but she let me know we'd meet soon enough. I had created the opportunity for that to happen by my thoughts and the request to visit the Sacred Valley.

Next morning, I realized I had been on an astral journey. But since I was about to visit Cuzco, I hoped to find the talking stone there.

When I shared my dream at breakfast, Yaya said she'd like to try communicating with stones when we got to the mountains. My parents said they would as well.

*At the Cuzco Airport*

# 4

## *At the Center of the Earth*

I was too excited to sit still as the taxi headed to the Lima airport. I had such a strong feeling I'd learn something important in Peru's valley of ancient magic.

The flight to Cuzco was amazing! We sailed above a sea of clouds that spread to infinity. Here and there, rising like islands above the cloud-sea, were silvery pyramids. They were the snowcaps of the Andes, the mountain range that spans western South America from north to south—the mountain range that shaped Peru's history.

The hour-long flight went so quickly I was still taking everything in when the pilot announced we were beginning our final descent to the Imperial City of the Incas. From the plane's window I could see that Cuzco was ringed by mountains. It was the rainy season, so the foothills of the mountains were a velvety green. Everything looked beautiful!

When we got off the plane I realized why Mother had made us wear warm clothes. Compared to Lima, Cuzco was cold. She also made us dress in layers because, while it could be cold at night and in the morning, it would get hot in the middle of the day.

After we claimed our bags, we boarded a bus to get to our hotel. It was full of people speaking many different languages. A man standing in the front of the bus held up a microphone and I thought he was going to sing. Instead he told us many facts about Cuzco. For one thing, it is nearly 11,000 feet above sea level but has pleasant weather because it's close to the equator. For another, the first Inca founded the city in the eleven hundreds so Cuzco is the oldest continuously inhabited city in South America.

The Inca Empire, he explained, was called Tahuantinsuyo. In Quechua, the language the Incas spoke, Tahuantinsuyo means Empire of the Four Cardinal Points. Cuzco, meaning the navel or center of the world, was the empire's capital. It had four main roads, one for each direction, and they extended from the center of the city to the corners of the Earth.

When it was built, Cuzco was laid out in a magical shape with the body of a puma and the head of a falcon. An animal sacred to the Inca, the puma's outline had been deliberately accentuated, perhaps so celestial beings would see it and know that people awaited them below.

The bus passed what the man called the imposing monument of the Inca king Pachacuti, whose name means earth shaker or world changer. Under his leadership and that of his son, the Inca Empire expanded to become the largest in pre-Hispanic America.

The man with the microphone finished by saying that Spanish invaders reached Cuzco in 1533. Although they tried, they never completely eliminated the city's Inca heritage. "Indeed," he said, "Pizarro and his fellow conquistadors might be astounded to learn that nowadays people come from all over the world just to see what they couldn't destroy."

Getting to our hotel became something of a challenge since it was on a narrow street, the bus was fairly wide, and traffic was heavy. At first the bustle was exciting, but then Yaya and I started having the headaches and stomach cramps Mother had warned us about. Our bodies were reacting to the altitude.

Thankfully, our hotel had a special coca leaf tea to relieve its effects. Mother explained that the coca plant is sacred to the Andean people and indigenous to these highlands. Coca leaves contain vitamins and minerals that expand the lungs and stimulate digestion, so the tea helps the body cope with the altitude. To do nothing when it starts affecting you can lead to a serious mountain sickness called soroche—definitely something to avoid.

"Breathing is an automatic process we seldom think about," said Father. "But when high altitude makes it hard to get enough oxygen, our bodies make a physical shift that alters our perceptions. As our bodies find new ways to balance and ground the circulatory and digestive systems, we become more aware of what's happening both inside us and around us."

After resting for a few hours and drinking lots of coca tea, we felt good enough to tackle the city. Since we'd be staying at high altitudes throughout our trip, my parents thought we should continue drinking the tea to prevent the onset of mountain sickness.

We rented a car and, with Father as our guide, drove to what had been the heart of the Inca city. It is now called the Plaza de Armas del Cuzco. Father explained that the people of the Tahuantinsuyo believed the Inca king was the son of Inti, their sun god. Public rituals to honor that divine lineage had been held on this wide, sunny plaza before the Spanish arrived.

One of the Catholic churches facing the plaza had been built on top of an Inca temple. I thought this was unusual, but as we drove around I learned that many Spanish-built churches and monasteries used the walls of Inca palaces or temples as their foundations. I looked carefully at each wall to see if it was the one from my dream.

Cuzco spreads across a wide, shallow valley and up the foothills of nearby mountains. Driving toward one of the foothills, we reached San Cristobal, a Catholic church built over Colcampata Palace. The palace had belonged to Manco Cápac, who founded Cuzco and began the Inca dynasty. Little is left of the palace, but what remains is preserved as an archeological site.

We walked around and saw an Inca wall to the right of the church. The wall had been intricately constructed with stones of different sizes, shapes, and colors. But its most important feature was a series of eleven niches, each topped with a large stone lintel. Too shallow to serve as shelters, the niches looked like doorways that had been purposely obstructed. Yaya asked why they'd been blocked off.

"They're blind doors," Father replied. "They don't open to any place in the physical world, but blind doors open into the spiritual world. The ancients made them partly as eye-catching structural elements and partly as portals to another dimension. In

Inca teachings, the hidden world figures just as prominently in this world as those doors fit into that wall."

"The Inca believed there were three planes of existence," he went on. "The first plane is Hanan Pacha, the upper world or heavens where celestial beings reside. Mountaintops are closer to that plane so that's where they built their shrines and temples. The middle plane is Kay Pacha or this world—our mundane, everyday existence on Earth. The third is Ukju Pacha, the inner world or underworld where ancestors, spirits of the dead, and underground or cave creatures dwell."

"When Incas entered a blind door," Yaya asked, "where did they think they were going?"

"Where do you think?" Father asked in reply.

"To the Ukju Pacha," Yaya said. "They went to the underworld."

The smile on Father's face confirmed that she was right.

In walking around, we passed several indigenous women selling handicrafts. They were wearing colorful multilayered skirts, wool cardigans, bright shawls, and brown felt fedoras. As they sat on the ground chatting, one was spinning wool into yarn from a spindle while another was carving a soapstone figure.

Mother went to examine the small animal sculptures displayed on a blanket before them. The animals had three basic forms: condor, puma, and serpent. Since we'd also seen them for sale at the hotel, Yaya asked if those three animals had some special meaning.

"They each stand for one of the Inca worlds," said Mother. "Where do you think the condor belongs?"

"The upper world," I answered.

"Yes, the Hanan Pacha," she clarified.

"And the puma?"

"Cucu Pacha," I said, making Yaya and mother laugh.

"Kay Pacha!" Mother replied. "What about the serpent?"

"Ukju Pacha!" Yaya exclaimed like a student who'd done her homework.

After taking some photos, we headed back to the car. To avoid overexertion, we were going to drive to Sacsayhuamán, a famous ruin at the upper part of the same archeological park.

*At Sacsayhuamán with Llamas*

# 5

# *The Stones at Sacsayhuamán*

We parked the car and walked onto a level field where a few llamas were grazing. Beyond them, three monumental stone ramparts—each over a thousand feet long—fortified the side of a hill and rose one above the other in a zigzag pattern emphasized by angular shadows. This was Sacsayhuamán, the Hill of the Falcon. It formed the head of Cuzco's puma outline and marked the upper limits of the original city. Father said it was also a huaca or holy place.

Beautiful buildings once stood at a ritual center above the ramparts but, after they became the center of an Inca uprising, the Spanish tore them down. Despite that, Sacsayhuamán is still a marvel. What remains are three terraces with walls made of stones too large for the Spanish to move—stones so large that some people even doubted humans had put them there.

The stones were gargantuan. Father pointed to one that was twenty-five feet high and weighed over a hundred tons. All had slightly rounded surfaces of polished gray andesite, a volcanic rock quarried nearby. In searching for my stone-friend, I saw that no two were alike. Not only were they different sizes, they were different shapes. Many had five, six, eight or more sides. Like a jigsaw puzzle, their irregular outlines fit tightly together. The stones were so precisely carved that nothing— not even a blade of grass—could be slipped between them.

Yaya and I had gone to get a close look at the stones, but at Father's urging we walked back to where we could take in the walls as a whole. I was impressed by how the stones' interlocking sides held the walls together without mortar. As if to call attention to that, the indented edges where stone met stone formed a pattern of shadows that stretched across each wall like a net.

The stones in the bottom wall were huge and distinctive. Those in the upper walls were a bit smaller and more uniform—and from a distance their curved surfaces and tight fit made me think of bread rolls that had melted together on a baking sheet.

When I told Yaya, she said they reminded her of the scales of a gigantic serpent. She had a point. There was something about the stones that made them seem alive….

Father directed us to the end of the bottom wall and showed us a ritual stone gate. There was one behind each wall. Mentioning that the upper terrace used to have three large towers, he asked us why this site might have had three walled terraces, three gates, and three towers.

"To represent the three worlds," Yaya and I replied almost in unison.

We slowly climbed to the top terrace. After taking in the view of Cuzco, we looked at the ground and saw the foundations of the towers the Spanish had removed. Despite that, Father said their essence remained and this was a good place to invoke a dome of protection. So he led us to the largest, the base of a round tower called Muyuc Marka. We walked to the center of its three concentric stone rings, sat in a circle, and joined hands.

Father explained that Cuzco and the Sacred Valley function as an energy hub for the planet. So, along with different perceptions caused by the altitude, he said we might experience unusual energies. Then he began an invocation: "We are going to enfold ourselves in a dome of light that will protect us so that nothing harmful happens to us, so that in the face of danger we will prevail, and so that we will experience peace and harmony."

After closing our eyes, we inhaled deeply and slowly, raised our arms, and held our breath for a short time. As we exhaled through our noses, we imagined a wonderful light descending from heaven to envelop and protect us.

With arms still raised, we slowly inhaled a second time. As we exhaled, we imagined the sun's energy beaming down and entering our bodies through the top of our heads. We lowered our arms to shoulder height and felt the healing sunbeams.

Inhaling for the final time, we visualized sunbeams lighting up our solar plexuses. We then exhaled as we dropped our arms and released our hands. When I opened my eyes, I saw a serene light encircling us.

Going down to the ceremonial plaza, we crossed to the Inca Throne, a stair-like set of platforms carved from a rocky outcrop. From the highest platform, Yaya and I saw that Sacsayhuamán's zigzags were mirror images of the jagged mountain peaks behind them.

From there we walked to the Chinkana—the place where one gets lost, a maze of interconnected caves. We explored a bit but didn't venture far into its tunnels. Supposedly part of a vast underground network linking many Inca sites, there are stories of people who disappeared into them, never to be seen again.

We had done a lot of walking for our first day in the high mountains but Father wanted us to experience one more archeological site. Just a short drive away, Q'enqo or zigzag place had been an astronomical observatory and the home of an oracle. Part of it had also been a ritual center devoted to making sacrifices and ceremonial offerings to Pachamama or Mother Earth.

In contrast to Sacsayhuamán's ramparts, where huge stones were brought from elsewhere to erect a wall, Q'enqo was carved from a limestone formation found there. It had been cut into a wonderland of tunnels, chambers, altars, niches, steps, and symbols—including zigzags.

Yaya and I went exploring. We found a large chamber and shouted to see if it had a good echo. It had a great one, so we started chanting Om and our parents joined us.

Father had taught us that Om was a simple sound with great meaning. Some people believe its sound was used to create the universe. So when Om is chanted over and over, it's as if the universe were being recreated and harmonized with sound.

After returning to our hotel, we wrote in our diaries and rested for a while. Then we showered and walked through streets lined with beautiful Inca stone walls. As we did, I realized that Inca walls were not all the same. Some had rough stones, some had smooth stones, and some were in between. Some had many-sided, slightly bulging stones arranged in jigsaw puzzle patterns. Others had nearly flat rectangles laid in neat rows like bricks. And others had irregular stones nicely arranged in random patterns. I studied them all, searching for my stone-friend. But there were so many walls and so many tourists and people selling things it was overwhelming.

I was relieved when we finally reached our destination, a quiet restaurant near the Plaza de Armas where we sat out of doors. We all had dieta de pollo, a chicken soup the waiter said would help our bodies adjust to the altitude. As we gazed at stars sparkling in the sky, a folkloric group played indigenous highland music that gave me chills of pleasure.

*On the Road to Pisac*

# 6

# *A Roadside Encounter*

We woke early on our second day. The weather was sunny and crisp—what people in the hotel described as a typical Cuzco day. Because Lima is on the Pacific coast, the radical change in altitude was still affecting us. So we just had a light breakfast and more coca tea.

Our plan was to visit Pisac, at the beginning of the Sacred Valley of the Incas, and then drive to a hotel in Urubamba. The first part of the trip involved a 20-mile drive, mostly on a mountainous road with no service stations. Since Father is really cautious, he made sure the car had gas, oil, and water. He even bought a tire, in addition to the spare already in the car, in case of an emergency.

Once outside the city, the car climbed a steep and sinuous road. On one side we looked up to eucalyptus forests and the ruins of ancient stone temples and palaces. On the other side, we looked down to Cuzco's red tile roofs that spread for miles across the valley toward the greens and purples of the mountains. On the horizon we saw snow-bright glaciers. Above was a dazzling blue sky. The vibrant landscape was breathtaking.

While he drove, Father pointed out Mount Ausangate, an imposing glacial peak 21,000 feet high that's quite visible throughout the region. Ausangate means revelation and this sacred mountain is home to a major Andean festival, Qoyllur Riti or Star of the Snow. The festival is held each year to honor the Apus, the spirit guardians of the mountains. Thousands of pilgrims travel from far and near bringing offerings. Barefoot and fasting, they climb through rocks and ice to reach the glacier. Many come down carrying huge blocks of ice as symbols of hope and renewal.

Despite some Christian aspects, the festival has deep roots in Peru's history. In addition to honoring the Apus, many participate to make amends for the failings that led to the downfall of the Inca

Empire and centuries of slavery, poverty, and misery. Many pilgrims also hope that being purified by the mountain's holy water will hasten the arrival of Inkarri—the last Inca king who, according to legend, will return at the end of times.

After driving for a while, we stopped along the road where a number of native artisans were selling crafts. There were also some pretty girls with lambs and llamas. The girls were nicely dressed in wool jackets decorated with ribbons and buttons and colorful, multilayered skirts. Flat hats with colorful trim topped their dark braids. The llamas had brightly colored yarn tassels on their ears and looked very picturesque. Father took a photo of Yaya and me with the girls and their lambs. He also took one of Mother with the llamas and paid the girls a price they had negotiated. Then we looked for souvenirs but didn't find anything to buy.

On our way back to the car I asked Mother why those girls got all dressed up and waited for tourists to take pictures of them. "Their parents are probably farmers," she replied. "Farmers don't make money until they sell their crops. But crops take time to grow and harvests don't happen every week, so modeling for photographs is one way those girls can earn money to help their families in between harvests."

"What do boys do?" Yaya asked. "And what about their parents?"

"Boys may watch the fields to keep birds and other animals from eating the produce. They may also gather firewood and work as shepherds or tourist guides," Mother replied. "Their mothers may weave or knit and they're the ones who usually sell the produce or crafts while their fathers work the fields or herd sheep and llamas in the mountains. Everyone in a farming family contributes what they can to make ends meet."

"Wow!" I exclaimed. "Yaya and I have it easy!"

"Yes, in a way," said Mother. "But in our way of life, your job is going to school. You and Yaya work really hard at learning."

We continued on to Pisac. Half an hour later we spotted an old car sitting on the side of the road. Father slowed down and observed that all the tires were in bad shape but one was completely destroyed. The vehicle was packed with highland elders and children. The driver and a woman who was probably his wife were sitting on the ground beside the damaged tire. He wore a poncho, long pants, and sandals. The woman had thick black braids, a round face, and beautiful bronze skin. She wore a wool jacket and colorful skirts. She also had a shawl over her shoulders and a brown fedora.

Father parked the car and went to ask the man if he needed help. The driver explained that the tire had hit a deep hole in the road and burst. They had no spare and without it they were stuck. As luck would have it, the extra tire father bought was just the right size for their car. So Father offered it to them, for which they were very grateful.

While Father and the driver changed tires, I could see the man's feet and asked Mother why his toes looked so beat-up. She explained that traditional highlanders went barefoot or wore sandals without socks in all sorts of weather. They live in mountainous places so their feet get roughed up from exposure. "Weathered feet," she concluded, "look different from ones that have always been protected by socks and shoes."

As Father headed back to our car, one of the elders gave him a multicolored sash as a token of gratitude. Father graciously accepted the gift and handed it to Mother when he got in the car. She studied the sash for a few minutes then passed it back to us.

Yaya asked if its woven shapes meant anything. Father took a quick look and said they were tocapus.

"What are topacus?" Yaya inquired.

"They're a type of symbolic writing, a system of Inca ideograms akin to Chinese pictograms," he explained. "Over eight-hundred different figures have been found on ancient ceramics and weavings, but their meanings are hidden in mystery."

"Do you think this sash has a message?" asked Yaya.

"If it does, my girl, I don't know what it says," Father replied and started the engine.

Mother suggested that Yaya and I take a nap because we would do a lot of hiking at the Inca sites in Pisac. I rested with my eyes closed for a while, wondering if I'd ever be able to fall asleep.

Apparently I did.

*Vendor with Sick Child in Pisac's Market*

# 7

## *Explorations in Pisac*

I awoke from my siesta to find the car descending into a wide agricultural valley that looked like a checkerboard of greens and browns.

Father explained that Pisac was at the eastern end of the Sacred Valley at about 1,500 feet lower than Cuzco. Running behind the town and along the whole north side of the valley were high mountains that stayed ice-covered year round. He pointed out a distant pair of glacial mountains, Pitusiray and Sahuasiray. They were the guardians of Huilkamayu, the Sacred River that flowed through the valley. That river is now called the Urubamba.

Mother added that Pisac was a picturesque town famous for its market held on Tuesdays, Thursdays and Sundays. Since it was Thursday, we'd get to see it.

Luckily, we found a place to park in town. Then, like everyone else seemed to be doing, we walked towards the market. We walked for some time along narrow streets where all the houses were whitewashed and had the same type of red clay tile roof, each topped with an iron cross.

The market was a kaleidoscope of colorful stalls that filled Pisac's central plaza and spilled into its side streets. Merchants had come from all over to sell produce as well as Andean crafts— ceramics, textiles, carvings, jewelry, leather goods, and clothing.

Most merchants were women and I found them and their outfits as interesting as what they were selling. Most market women were not dressed in Sunday clothes like the girls Father had photographed or many of the women we'd seen in Cuzco. With a few exceptions, they were wearing what looked like work clothes.

All or nearly all of them wore two braids as well as a full skirt, a cardigan sweater, a fedora, and sandals made from recycled tire treads. Many wore aprons over their skirts and sat on the ground. Others, probably shoppers, walked around with colorful shawls slung over their backs in which they carried either produce or a child. A small number of women wore colorful multilayered skirts that Mother called polleras.

A few women wore flat hats covered by what looked like small, fringed tablecloths decorated with embroidered designs. Mother called them monteras—as she did the wide-brimmed women's hats shaped like hubcaps. The crown of the hubcap style was often divided into quarters by ribbons and rickrack and decorated with colored fabric in geometric shapes.

When I asked why the women wore such unusual hats, Mother explained that a woman's hat usually identified what village she came from. For men, ponchos and sometimes hats identified their home village. But no one in the market had on a poncho.

There was a great variety of textiles for sale: machine-loomed rugs, blankets, ponchos, and wall hangings; hand-woven ponchos and belts; and colorful, hand-knit sweaters, hats, belts, gloves, and scarves. The more expensive items were made from lamb and llama wool. The less expensive ones were made from acrylic. The finest and most expensive ones used alpaca. After farming and tourism, textile making has been Peru's most important industry.

We went from textiles to the produce section, which seemed just as varied and just as colorful. There were carrots and olives, beans and potatoes. Potatoes are native to the highlands and the varieties for sale came in many different colors. So did the maize. Since it wasn't corn season, most merchants were selling dried corn on the cob in colors that ranged from white and pale yellow to maroon and a dark bluish-purple. But then we found the exception.

Outdoor food vendors were selling Pisac's celebrated choclo con queso—boiled ears of nutty, large-kernel, pale Andes corn served with slices of white farmer's cheese. We didn't expect to find fresh maize at this time of year and couldn't resist such a treat. It was simply delicious.

After that we walked around to different merchants, comparing prices and the quality of various items. Easygoing and friendly, the people lacked the sort of edginess and loneliness one finds in Lima, so we were enjoying everything about the people and the place.

In one corner of the plaza we observed a woman vendor with several young children. The infant strapped to her back looked unnaturally flushed and the woman looked troubled. Mother said the child seemed feverish so she got out a small first aid kit. Discretely dousing a clean handkerchief with rubbing alcohol, she gave it to the woman to put on the ailing child's forehead. Mother also gave her a mild fever remedy and explained how to use it. When she bought a few things, the woman was so grateful she kissed Mother's hand.

We continued shopping, buying little souvenirs for our grandmothers, cousins, aunts, and uncles. With gifts in hand, we returned to the car and headed up the mountain toward Inca Pisac, the archeological park from which the market town derives its name.

The car went up a steep and winding road bordered on the right by eucalyptus trees, fields of produce, herds of livestock, clusters of adobe buildings, and waterfalls tumbling from the glaciers above. On the left was a precipice that grew scarier as we climbed.

After some hairpin switchbacks, the road ran along a narrow ridge to a plateau with a parking area and the entrance to the Inca Pisac site. From the observatory 2,000 feet above it, we had an extraordinary view of the agricultural valley, the precipitous mountainsides stepped with gracefully curved agricultural terraces, and a cliff honeycombed with caves across the gorge.

To reach different sections of the park, we had to hike single file along a cliff-hugging Inca path. Level sections were made of packed earth but whenever the path climbed or descended a slope there were stone steps—too numerous to count. A fear of heights made the hike a real challenge for me. But I'd requested the trip and couldn't let my fear keep me from reaching the ruins. So I walked between Father and Mother and tried not to look down.

The path rose and fell and twisted as the day grew warm. Going up and down so many steps was tiring but we took our time and rested now and then. When we finally reached the residential area called Pisaqa, it was worth the effort. Named for partridges that still inhabit the region, thirty really fine stone buildings had been erected there for the Inca king and his entourage.

I looked for my stone-friend as we walked among the graceful buildings. They made me feel calm and close to nature. So I knew what Father meant when he pointed out how well Inca buildings were integrated into the natural landscape.

From there, we climbed to the ceremonial and scientific center just below the mountain's rocky peak, a center named for its intihuatana. The Quechua word means the place where time stops, but it's often called the sun's hitching post. This was one of the locations where the Incas made astronomical observations. Studying the sun, moon, and stars helped them predict the weather and establish seasonal and festival calendars vital to their farming culture.

Father said this was a very holy place. Made from beautiful pink granite, the stonework on the temples was better than at Pisaqa. Most remarkable was the Intihuatana itself, a huge natural outcropping enshrined within a wall of curved ashlars. Despite damaged carvings on its surface, the stone was powerful. I never imagined a stone could have such strong energy!

When Father went off to take some photos, Mother, Yaya and I wandered among the buildings. All of a sudden, I had a yearning to feel into the Intihuatana using the process I learned from Ojito when I met the talking stone.

Mother and Yaya agreed to join me, so we found a spot where we could sit facing the megalith and began taking slow, deep breaths. After a while we touched the great stone with our hands and foreheads, trying to sense its history and receive its messages.

I became aware that the stone was asking me something… asking if I understood what it means to hold time.

"Probably it means to stop it," I responded, "or not let it continue."

"In ancient days, it was a turning point that showed the universe was subject to cycles," said the Intihuatana. "Together with natural disasters and great planetary changes, each of Pachamama's cycles ends so that a new one can begin."

"You yourself are subject to cycles," the great stone added. "Your birthday marks the end of one cycle and the start of another. Something about that new cycle brought you here—something beyond mere coincidence."

"Of course!" I exclaimed aloud. Just as I grasped the Intihuatana's meaning, I recalled something Ojito taught me: there's no such thing as a chance encounter and things happen when the time is right.

When I refocused, the stone explained that this was a special time of learning. I and my family and many others would come to know important things.

Just then, Mother asked if I was okay. I opened my eyes and saw a worried look on her face. My outburst had ended the meditation for Mother and Yaya, so I apologized.

"No problem, love," said Mother, "but we should thank the Intihuatana." So we did.

When Father rejoined us, we hiked down to a place where we could sit in the shade. Mother got cheese sandwiches and fruit from her bag and we had a picnic as falcons soared above us.

Mother wanted to internally process what had happened, so she suggested that we not talk about our experience with the Intihuatana until we finished eating. Once we did, we had a lively conversation. Mother said she had a great sense of connectedness to the world and everything in it—even stones. Yaya reported feeling as spacious as the galaxies. Since neither had a conversation with it, they wanted to hear about mine.

Father was intrigued by the idea that now was a special time of learning for us all. When I mentioned that the Intihuatana said something about cycles ending and beginning together with disasters, he remarked, "The Inca people thought of time as cyclical. We generally think of time as linear but on one level we still see the year as cyclical, just as they did, because seasons have a repeating pattern.

"Here the wet season runs from November to April. The dry season runs from April to October. The cycle goes from wet to dry, wet to dry, and so on. Each wet season may vary from the year before, but it's still the rainy time of year with predictable patterns of movement in the heavenly bodies, especially the sun and Milky Way. If the year is a cycle, it's easy to see time as a cycle."

"Why don't we?" I asked.

"Writing was a factor," he explained. "The Bible helped shape Western ideas of time and history. Because of it, we see time as linear and sequential. Having a linear sense of time encourages us to see history as forward-moving and improving.

"But those who picture time as cyclical understand history as repeating patterns. Things will change like the seasons do, but that doesn't mean they'll improve. The conquistadors, for example, were agents of change. Their arrival was interpreted as a pachacuti by the Incas."

"I thought Pachacuti was the ruler who expanded the Empire," said Yaya.

"You're right," Father replied. "He adopted the word for earthquake as his name and a symbol for his role—and he changed his world in a way that was good for the Incas. However, the word pachacuti also means a disaster that marks the end of an era. In the Inca view of time, both good and dark times end. At some point, the dark times that began with the Spanish invasion will end and a new age will begin. The Q'ero, the most traditional of highlanders, say the new era will see the return of Inkarri, the last Inca king. With Inkarri comes the end of times."

Worried he might say no, I asked, "Is that a good thing?"

"Yes, my love," he replied. "The Q'ero see the end of times as an era of integration, an era of healing."

*The Elder from the Mountain*

# 8

## *What the Guardian Says*

Mother and Father were engaged in conversation, so Yaya and I went to explore the area. All at once she started climbing a steep slope toward a cave she spotted. I wanted to follow but my fear of heights held me back. As I watched Yaya disappear into the cave, however, my curiosity got stronger than my fear and I set off after her.

It was a difficult climb. My feet kept slipping on loose pebbles and my heart raced wildly. It was only by sheer willpower that I made it to the entrance of the cave and quickly stepped inside so I wouldn't have to see how far I was above the ground.

Surprisingly large and deep, the cave was not as dark as I expected. I could clearly see that it was lined with walls made of stone and adobe that formed a series of small rooms, some of which had crumbled walls. I found Yaya digging among the stones in one of those broken rooms. She pointed to a human skull in a wall niche and said, "I put that where it belongs."

"This is an Inca burial site!" Yaya exclaimed. "Mummies were put in these little rooms along with food and personal stuff so they wouldn't get restless and bother the living. From here the dead could watch over the land, the crops, and their relatives like guardian angels."

I was feeling a bit uneasy with the energy in the cave when the whole place filled with flapping wings. "Look at the birds!" I cried as dark shapes zoomed about.

"They're bats!" Yaya cried. "Watch out!"

We ducked as the bats flew out through the mouth of the cave. In the quiet that followed, we heard a gentle, authoritative voice say, "You must respect this place."

Yaya and I froze in fright. We looked in every direction, trying to figure out who was speaking but saw no one. Finally, after what felt like a long time, a little old woman emerged from the shadows at the back of the cave. She had gray braids and wore a long dark skirt with a patterned hem. She looked really old but moved toward us in a graceful glide—almost like a dancer.

"Señora, we're sorry to bother you," Yaya apologized. "We didn't mean to offend you or the ancestors."

"Your presence is not a problem," the old woman said. "You are high-spirited yet respectful. However over the years, many people have robbed and looted these caves. Dismayed by such conduct, we withdrew. As a result, young people lost contact with their ancient traditions.

"See how bones have been scattered about the floor by thieves and vandals?" she continued. "For profits or thrills they destroy our sacred things and show contempt for our values. This is the work of people who neither love themselves nor respect others."

"We're not here to steal anything!" Yaya said uneasily. "We want to know its history."

"I understood that," the old woman replied, "from the careful way you picked up the bones and put them in their proper places."

Feeling we should introduce ourselves, I said, "Señora, I am Tanis. This is my sister Yearim. We live in Lima and our parents brought us here on vacation."

"I am pleased to meet you."

"With your permission, Señora," I ventured, "why did the ancient ones bury their dead in high mountain caves?"

"A mountaintop is closer to the Hanan Pacha," she replied, "what you call the upper world. And caves are thresholds or passages between worlds. Our ancestors emerged from caves after traveling through the underworld where they survived great cataclysms."

"Like the Ayar brothers?" Yaya asked.

I wanted to know who they were but this was not the time to ask.

"There are other reasons as well," the old woman continued. "We place our mummies in a cave to sow the seeds of future life. When our people cross—what you call dying—they return to the womb of Pachamama for rebirth. Putting them in a cave is like planting a seed so it can sprout.

"The living have an important role in this process," she added. "To help Mother Earth realize she is pregnant and needs to give birth to new people, the living must be reborn in mind and spirit. Spiritual growth does not occur in the hereafter; it comes about in day-to-day life as you work for the good of everyone—not just yourself. Each day, the living must do as the ancestors taught: they must find life's magic through love.

"Right now, your steps are being guided by the Apus, spirit guardians of the mountains. Soon you will visit Ollantaytambo. Our ancient ways have been kept unchanged for centuries there. All the right conditions are in place for meeting with the Council of Wisdom Elders.

"When a spiritually evolved, reincarnated person enters the Sacred Valley," she went on, "members of that Council know it and come down from the mountains to meet that person. Once the necessary elements are in place, a Council member will give you an important message." And with that, the old woman vanished.

Full of feelings and questions about the old woman and what she said, Yaya and I stood stock-still for a minute or so. Then we went to find our parents. However, we first had to descend the slope. I was glad for Yaya's help because going down was much harder that going up.

When our parents first saw us they looked relieved. Then we got a scolding. "Girls, where have you been?" Father demanded. "We were quite worried and have been looking all over for you."

"We're sorry," Yaya exclaimed breathlessly. "You won't believe what happened! We were exploring a cave of tombs when an old woman appeared and said we'd get a message in Ollantaytambo."

"You should never do such things alone!" Father scolded. "It's too risky. The terrain can be dangerous and you could have had an accident."

Mother asked, "What sort of message?"

"I don't know," I replied. "The old woman said we'd meet teachers in Ollantaytambo."

Father looked distressed. "Girls, stop imagining things!" he said.

"It's not something we imagined, Father!" insisted Yaya. "An old woman told us about the message. She wore clothes from long ago—I saw some like hers in the anthropology museum."

Father considered us gravely and then said it was time to return to the car. As we were gathering our things, I suddenly remembered the Ayar brothers and asked what they had to do with caves.

"The Ayars are the mythic ancestors of the Inca," replied Mother. "There are different versions of their story and your father tells a long one with many good details. There's no time for it now, so I'll give you a short account of how Manco Cápac founded Cuzco."

"What about the cave?"

"I'm getting to that, my love," she explained. "Manco Cápac's original name was Ayar Manco. He had three younger brothers named Ayar Auca, Ayar Uchu and Ayar Cachi. Along with their four sister-wives, the four brothers were sent by their heavenly father to help the people of this world. At that time, people lived like wild beasts without laws nor agriculture."

Seeing the question in my face, Mother said, "Here's where the cave comes in. After traveling for a long time through the underworld, the four brothers and four sisters came into this world through a cave on a hillside. The hill had three caves that were like windows into the Earth. Many accounts specify that the Ayars emerged from the middle cave, a place called Pacaritampu—Inn of Dawn or House of Origin.

"The sisters and brothers wanted good land for farming. As they searched, they travelled from place to place. But Ayar Cachi abused his magical powers so much that his brothers had to confine him to a cave where he turned into stone."

"A cave like the one Yaya and I were in?" I asked, trying to imagine the details.

"Perhaps..." she replied. "The other brothers journeyed on. Before long, Ayar Uchu got trapped in a crevice and Ayar Auca turned into a bird. In time, like Ayar Cachi, both became stones. Their transformation allowed the three stone-brothers to guide their human siblings. When Ayar Manco reached what is now Cuzco, he changed his name to Manco Cápac, built a city there, established a code of laws, and taught people how to grow maize. With his sister-wife Mama Ocllo, he ruled for many years."

Having finished, Mother indicated it was time to head down the path—a trek that would demand our full attention. "Now we should go," she said.

It was late afternoon by the time we reached the car and I was glad we didn't have to walk any more. Father was grateful we didn't have to cross a mountain pass. We would drive twenty-five miles along the valley to Urubamba, which was at about the same elevation as Pisac.

When we reached the highway, the car was inundated by a downpour that made it hard to see, so Father pulled off the road. As we waited for the rain to pass, my parents asked many questions about what had happened in the cave. I even drew a picture of the old woman. Father concluded that she might have been the spirit guardian of the mountain. Mother agreed, saying, "Perhaps she's an Elder from the Mountain." Once the shower ended, we continued on to Urubamba.

I fell asleep right after dinner and spent all night dreaming about the cave and the old woman. In my dream, however, she told me about a lake near Cuzco where people saw strange lights as well as large, extraordinary birds.

*The Temple Wall at Ollantaytambo*

# 9

## *Our Time in Ollantaytambo*

It was chilly when we got up and the early daylight was blocked by mountains, so the valley stayed dark until the sun climbed over them—then it seemed like a light had been switched on. The air got warm, the sky grew luminous, and the glacial peaks around Urubamba glistened.

The hotel's dining room was full of tourists from all around the world. Besides coca tea, we had a typical regional breakfast of warm bread with fresh butter, white cheese, and locally grown black Azupa olives.

After that, we headed toward Ollantaytambo. The drive along the Urubamba River was only twelve miles but seemed like forever because Yaya and I were eager to get our special message.

Gazing out the windows, we saw farmers plowing small fields with oxen. Most of the flat land and low mountainside terraces were covered with a patchwork of barley, bean, lentil, maize, and wheat fields. High up the mountainsides, terraces were planted with potato, oca, and quinoa. Weeds, small bushes, and an occasional tree divided one field from another, and since nearby fields were planted with different crops, there were variations in color and texture.

Out of the blue, Yaya informed us that this valley had been Peru's breadbasket since the time of the Incas. Father agreed. But when I asked how she knew, she simply said, "Social studies."

"Did you learn why the valley has been so productive?" asked Father.

"It's a mix of things," she replied. "The valley's near the equator yet has a high elevation so its climate is more temperate than tropical. But the main thing was the Inca were great farmers and engineers. The mountains around the valley trap sun-warmed air and protect the crops from cold winds, but they also block the rain. So the Inca used irrigation and terracing to deal with that and carefully bred plants and animals to thrive here."

"That's a good summary," Father remarked. "The tasty large-kernel choclo we ate in Pisac is an example of their selective breeding and some scholars say more types of plants—edible and medicinal—were domesticated in Peru than anywhere else on Earth."

Still impatient to reach our destination, Yaya and I diverted ourselves by trying to identify the shrubs and trees we spotted from the car. It was easy to recognize Spanish broom, the bushy gold-flowered weed that grew in such profusion by the side of the road. It would have been hard to miss the tall, slender eucalyptus that forested some hillsides or grew single-file between farmer's fields. And we noticed some avocado trees near farmers' houses. But the most splendid tree, one sacred to the Inca, was the wide-canopied pisonay whose scarlet flowers can only be pollinated by hummingbirds.

When the valley began to narrow, we were nearing our destination. Located at the western end of the Sacred Valley where the Patacancha River flows into the Urubamba, Ollantaytambo sits on a slope beneath a 3,000-foot cliff. It has South America's oldest continuously occupied buildings and was the site of a 1537 battle in which the Incas defeated the Spanish.

Developed in the mid-fourteen-hundreds by the Inca king Pachacuti, the town was laid out as a grid of streets enclosing a vast central plaza. After the conquistadors regained possession of the town, a new plaza was created at the town's southern end. That's where we were headed.

Surprisingly, the paved highway ended abruptly just before it reached Ollantaytambo. Without warning, it became a cobblestone street that grew narrower as it climbed towards town. Traffic got increasingly chaotic as we drew near the plaza. When we finally arrived, it was so jammed with tourist buses that Father drove directly to the archeological park on the far side of town.

After we got out of the car, Mother tied the elder's gift sash like a headband across my forehead. With a similar one she bought in Pisac, she did the same to Yaya, saying they made us look distinctive. We'd be easy to spot in a crowd.

The ruins of Ollantaytambo loomed above us as we walked outside the park's entrance. There were merchants everywhere, selling all sorts of arts and crafts. Some were even selling stuff they called antique—things Father said were actually recently made.

We entered the park to face sixteen formidable stepped terraces. Their beige granite stones were not as big as those at Sacsayhuamán and their walls were not as high, but the Ollantaytambo terraces made me feel really small and I mentioned that to Father.

"There's a good reason for that," he replied. "The wall on the bottom terrace is about six feet high, and from where we stand each terrace appears to be the same height. That's because the walls increase in height as they go up. The top ones reach ten feet or more. Were they all the same, the upper terraces would look increasingly short. Our bodies feel this... and our minds don't know why. Considering how steep the terraces are and how far up they go, some sense of awe and humility—a sense of feeling small—was surely the intended effect."

In contrast to Pisac's graceful terraces that followed the contours of the mountain, these looked straight as a ruler. Yaya said they reminded her of Mayan pyramids.

A long stairway with over two hundred steps was the only way to the ceremonial area above those terraces. Its stone steps were intentionally steep but Yaya and I climbed them at a near run, while our parents dawdled, pacing themselves and enjoying the views from different terraces.

We met at the Temple of the Sun. Apparently under construction when the Spanish arrived, it's still unfinished. We saw the roughed-in shape of the main courtyard where ceremonies would have been held under an open sky. The yard was littered with huge ashlars called weary stones because they were lying down—too tired to make it to their final destination.

At the rear of the courtyard stood a marvelous wall oriented toward the rising sun. Made of warm, rose-colored granite, it had six megaliths with five narrow shims between them. Each megalith was thirteen or so feet high and five to six feet wide. The shims, each made of several sections of the same rose granite, probably served as earthquake shock absorbers. Similar shims had been found in temples near Lake Titicaca, but this construction method was unique among Inca stonework in the Sacred Valley.

A couple of megaliths had faintly visible reliefs of a stepped geometric form that resembled a chakana, an Inca symbol also known as the Andean cross. And the partially disfigured head of a puma protruded from another.

"This wall," Father explained, "reveals a great deal about how the Inca regarded stone. For them, stone had an essence or kamay that was independent of its form. Stones were sacred but their holiness was embedded in their material—not their form. So stones like these that formed a temple wall were as sacred to the Inca as whatever was inside the temple."

We moved closer to connect with the wall. Breathing slowly and deeply, we closed our eyes and placed our foreheads and hands on the stones. Father urged us to imagine a tunnel in our foreheads and suggested we propel ourselves through it in a clockwise direction—going through days, months, years, and centuries back to the time of the Incas.

Little by little I could feel the vibration of the stone's history. I was getting a sense of the people who worked it and their purpose for building the wall. I began going deeper, feeling stronger sensations, when a sudden flash broke my connection.

I opened my eyes at the same time Yaya, Mother, and Father did. A Japanese man had taken a photo of us. With our chance to commune with the wall disrupted, we moved on.

Behind the wall was a huge outcrop around which two other walls had been erected. Between that boulder and the back of the rose granite wall, we found an underground passage that Inca priests had probably used. Then we climbed agricultural terraces contoured to the steep cliff-like side of the mountain.

The site was vast and, for some reason, exploring it required a great deal of physical effort and more energy than we had. The altitude and our interrupted connection with the wall may have been factors in our low energy level, but Yaya and I were also disappointed that we hadn't encountered the teacher who would give us a message.

On our way out of the archeological zone, we passed the Baño de la Ñusta, a ritual water basin and font at the foot of the terraces. Yaya asked what a ñusta was.

"In Inca society, ñustas were the princess-daughters of the Inca king," Father explained. "They were also young women called the Chosen Ones who lived as cloistered nuns in service to the divine sun. In the natural world, Ñustas are water spirits that complement the Apus or mountain spirits. Ñustas and Apus have a yin-yang connection."

"What does yingyang mean?" I asked.

"Yin-yang," he said, "is a Chinese term used to explain how things that seem to be opposites—night and day, female and male, fluid water and solid stone—are actually interconnected in the natural world."

I liked having things be connected and was now very curious about the Baño de la Ñusta, so I walked closer.

There had been ritual baths or water temples at each site we visited and there were fountains among the terraces above, but this one, set against a rustic wall, seemed very special. It featured a huge gray granite boulder with rough, unfinished sides. Carved on its front were three overlapping sets of steps that looked like a bridge. A steady stream of clear water from deep within the mountain flowed across the flat top of the bridge and cascaded into a pool. Over time, the pool's sides had been worn smooth by the hands and feet of uncountable numbers of people.

We all gratefully cupped our hands in the cold water and put some on our faces and necks to cool off. Then Yaya and I took off our shoes and socks and splashed our feet in the pool.

Revived and suddenly famished, we headed to town to get something to eat. We had to walk quite a way. Near the new plaza we found a small restaurant. It was a bit touristy but the food was good. Yaya and Mother ordered grilled trout with baked purple potatoes. Father and I ordered a salad of boiled yellow potatoes, hard-cooked eggs, and large black olives in a spicy cheese sauce.

I was still looking for my stone-friend so I studied the walls as we strolled around the plaza after lunch. We passed a colonial church made with Inca stones and I was surprised by how it made me feel. Instead of the sense of harmony I got from Inca masonry, its careless stonework created a feeling of chaos inside me.

We came across a statue of the Inca general Ollanta, after whom the city is named, and Father asked if we wanted to hear a romantic story about him. We quickly said yes.

"Long ago," he began, "Ollanta was a general in service to the Inca king Pachacuti. In the mid-fourteen-hundreds, under Ollanta's brilliant military leadership, the Incas expanded their empire by conquering adjacent populations. Grateful for his service, Pachacuti promised the victorious general anything he wanted.

"Ollanta was deeply in love with the ruler's daughter, princess Cusi Coyllar. She had stolen his heart and he had stolen hers in return. Theirs was a truly reciprocal love. But it was also a secret because Inca law forbade anyone except Inca descendants to marry a person of royal Inca blood. Ollanta was of high rank, but he was not a direct descendant of the Inca. So when Pachacuti promised Ollanta anything he wanted, the general put his life on the line and asked for the one thing he wanted most—to marry the woman he loved. Pachacuti refused.

"When Cusi heard this she was heartbroken and vowed to marry no one else. In response, her angry father confined her to the cloister for Chosen Women—a place no man save the ruler was allowed to enter.

"Feeling betrayed because Pachacuti had broken his word and imprisoned Cusi, Ollanta fled from Cuzco and started a rebellion that lasted ten years. In the end, he was captured by means of trickery. Along with his fellow rebels, Ollanta was put into prison.

"Before long, Pachacuti died. His son, Túpac Yupanqui, became the new king. Since he needed the rebels' military help to expand the Empire even more, Túpac released them all and promoted Ollanta to major general.

"Túpac then discovered that his sister, Cusi Coyllar, was alive and went to free her. The first thing Cusi did was ask about Ollanta. Hearing that he was alive and well, Cusi told her brother of the great love she and Ollanta had for each other and all they had endured because of it. Túpac was so moved that he allowed them to marry."

Once Father finished, Yaya and I couldn't help sighing. Mother smiled and hugged us both simultaneously.

The area around the plaza was packed with tourists, so we kept going until we found streets with mostly local people. As we walked, we became enchanted by this place from another era. Its buildings were older than anything Yaya and I had ever seen. Its cobblestone streets were built centuries before the invention of automobiles and, though straight, many were too narrow for a car to pass through. Water ran swiftly along the side or down the middle of each street in a narrow stone trench that directed glacial melt or rainwater downhill. And people moved slower than they do in Lima.

In the Inca-built section of town, street corners were marked with huge cut stones. And the long east-west streets were bordered on both sides by old stone buildings and walls that ran without a break from corner to corner. There were no sidewalks, so the high walls on both sides made the narrow streets feel like tunnels.

Originally there had been only one doorway on each city block. Opening into a large communal courtyard, such doorways had large single-stone lintels and what Father called the distinctly Inca trapezoid—meaning its sides leaned in so the top was narrower than the bottom. Its trapezoidal shape and single-stone lintel enabled the doorway to withstand the region's frequent earthquakes.

Trapezoidal doorways also identified this as the hanan part of the city, an area for the ruling elites. Like every Inca city, Ollantaytambo had been divided into two parts: a hanan or upper section and a hurin or lower section. Farmers were in the servant class so they would have lived in the hurin section.

During our wanderings, we come across an old donkey loaded with sacks of livestock feed, followed by a man wearing a nearly shapeless fedora, a white shirt, loose brown pants, rubber sandals, and a brown poncho folded over one shoulder because the sun was so hot he didn't need it now. We smiled and nodded our heads and the donkey's owner gave us a gracious smile—the response local people generally gave us.

Here and there we saw a red bag hanging from a pole on the side of a building. The red bag indicated that the place sold chicha de jora, a popular home-brewed corn beer. And we found no shortage of barking dogs, though some were frightening when they followed us for too long.

We passed a doorway as two elderly women entered it. Each had long braids and wore a white long-sleeve blouse, a dark ankle-length skirt with a multicolored hem, a shawl, sandals, and the same type of fedora. I whispered excitedly to Mother that, except for their hats, those women were dressed like the Elder from the Mountain. "That's the clothing style of older tradition keepers," she remarked.

"Why do those women or the ones we saw in polleras and monteras wear such old-fashioned clothes?" I asked.

"When it's combined with speaking their language and practicing ancient rituals, wearing traditional styles of clothing preserves their sense of who they are," Mother said.

Father nodded. "Many here in Ollantaytambo and farther up the mountains quietly maintain customs that honor the old ways."

"That's what the Elder from the Mountain said," Yaya declared. "She told us that down through the centuries Ollantaytambo had faithfully followed the ancient ways."

We continued walking until at some point Father said, "I've been mulling over the idea of what clothing meant to the Incas. Their myths say that one reason Inti sent his children to Earth was to teach people to make and wear clothes to distinguish themselves from wild animals. So the Incas wore fine weavings to demonstrate how civilized they were—and the Inca king made daily sacrifices of the finest weavings to Inti.

"For centuries," he continued, "the highland Quechua, who are the descendants of the Inca, have regarded weaving as essential for survival. It also conveys both cultural and personal meanings. Ancient design patterns, such as tocapus, use a communal symbol system; and garments, such as ponchos, follow established forms; yet each piece of hand-woven clothing was unique. So their clothing has many levels of meaning."

"Don't our clothes mean something?" Yaya asked.

"Of course they do," he replied, "but our mass-produced clothes don't have deep cultural roots. And when they're used in a kind of rivalry to show who's richer or cooler or part of the in-crowd, they result in social segregation. In contrast, traditional clothes are more often used to foster a sense of community. As your mother explained, the highlanders' traditional clothing, rituals, and language preserve their sense of who they are."

"I still don't understand," I said.

"I'll give you an example from history," Father said. "In 1572 Spanish authorities killed the last Inca king, Túpac Amaru. For the next two hundred years, colonial authorities enslaved most of Peru's native people. Even though there were many rebellions before it, none threatened the Spanish hold on Peru as much as the one in 1780. That year Túpac Amaru II, a descendant of the last Inca king, set off a major rebellion that took the Spanish colonial government six months to crush. Once they did, colonial authorities outlawed all native traditions—clothes included, and even banned the Quechua language."

When I asked why, he said, "To erase their history. By forcing the natives to dress, pray, and speak like Spaniards, colonial authorities hoped to wipe away all traces of their Inca heritage. The suppression was so severe that many natives complied by adopting the foreign ways. But others resisted by making largely outward changes—modifying their clothing yet keeping some Inca elements, accepting Christianity without abandoning their Earth-honoring practices, and speaking Spanish in public but Quechua at home.

"Remarkably, the highlanders managed to withstand that and later attempts to destroy their historic identity," he added. "And they were greatly helped by the mountains."

"How did the mountains help?" I asked.

"From a logical perspective, the very remoteness of the mountains kept the highlanders out of sight and out of the minds of colonial officials," he explained. "But logic is narrow and the world is wide. From a magical perspective, the Apus protected those who kept the old ways. Either way you look at it, the mountains helped."

I told Father I liked the magical explanation. He gave me a wink and replied, "So do I, but a logical back-up is handy if people aren't bilingual."

All at once Yaya dashed ahead. Bowing to a stone wall, she asked, "Parlez vous la magique?" Then she stood up, put her hands on her hips, and added, "Or do you only speak logic?" For some reason we all found that quite funny. And because of it, I finally got Father's point that logic and magic are like different languages based on different ways of understanding the world.

Eventually we reached the southern edge of town and saw a mountain with huge Inca buildings high up its slope. Though they looked as big and as striking as cathedrals, they were qollqas or granaries for harvested produce and storehouses for other supplies.

Father called the granaries engineering marvels. They were positioned at such high altitudes because food could be preserved better in cooler air. The particular placement of their windows allowed sufficient airflow to prevent spoilage. And putting gravity as well as the mountainside itself to good use, new produce was added at the top of the building while older produce was removed from the bottom.

When I asked why they needed to store so much food, Yaya said, "I read that Inca kings kept food so they could redistribute it after natural disasters like frosts, droughts, and floods."

"That's right," said Father. "The qollqa was a food bank. When crops in a certain area were destroyed, Inca officials loaned food to the affected people. But they were expected to pay it back from the surplus of good years."

On the side of the same mountain, we also observed the gigantic carving of a man's face. Some say it's the face of Wiracochan, a creator-god who came before Viracocha. Others say it's the face of Chimpaccahua, the legendary man who looks straight ahead. We only looked. We'd done enough climbing for that day.

Heading back towards our car, we saw an elderly local woman dressed like the two we'd seen earlier—except she carried a child on her back in a big colorful sling. In passing, we smiled and she returned the smile. Then she stopped and stared at my forehead.

My headband seemed to interest her, so I explained how I got it. I wasn't sure how much she understood because I only speak Spanish and Mother had warned me earlier that some highland people only speak Quechua. Her eyes grew wide. Then she smiled and walked away as we continued toward the car.

A few minutes later she called out to us and we turned around. Still carrying the child, she was now accompanied by a very old man. We waited for them to reach us. As they approached, I noticed that the man carried himself with much dignity. I also noticed his clothes: a weathered fedora, dark pants, sandals, a vest, and a wide belt with a woven pattern.

The venerable man greeted us in Spanish. Then he grew silent and gazed at us so intensely it made us uneasy. Finally Father asked, "Señor, is something wrong?"

"Pardon me," the old man replied. "I do not mean to be rude. I'm curious to know if you are you the people who helped the family with the flat tire on the road from Cuzco to Pisac?"

Father said yes and the man asked, "Are you the family who helped a woman with a sick child in Pisac? And did you enter a cave in the mountain near Pisaqa?"

"Yes," Mother answered. "I did what had to be done to help the child. Our daughters entered the cave but their intentions were good. I hope we caused no offence…. How do you know all this?"

"I can see it in your poq'po, Señora," replied the old man. "Your poq'po shines pink and green—exceptionally bright. It shows that you are good and generous. Your whole family looks the same. That is good, very good."

I had no idea what a poq'po was and was about to ask the old man when he said, "How do I know? Here in the valley everything is known. Everything!"

Then he apologized, "Please forgive me. I have forgotten my manners. Allow me to introduce myself. My name is José Choque. This is my wife, Juana, and my grandson, Tomasito."

"It's a pleasure to meet you, Don José," Father said warmly. "We are namesakes, since I am also José. This is my wife, Aida, and my daughters, Yearim and Tanis." Father finished his introduction with a handshake.

"Will you do us the honor of having dinner at our house?" Doña Juana inquired.

Uncertain of what to do, my parents looked at each other. They did not want to be a burden but they knew that declining such an invitation might give offense. Finally, Father said, "It would be our pleasure!"

We followed them a short distance to a trapezoidal stone doorway with a large stone lintel. Its antique wooden door opened into a courtyard. On one side was a garden where hens and chicks wandered. Opposite the garden was an area where stones had been sorted and piled. Beyond that was a two-story house made of stone.

Once inside, we passed through the kitchen to a large living-dining room. As she directed us to the dining table, Doña Juana lit a kerosene lamp to supplement the room's electric light bulbs.

Doña Juana and Don José left us alone with Tomasito, who watched us intently until his attention shifted to a plastic car on the table. He grabbed it and made engine sounds with evident pleasure as he played. Then a wheel fell off and he got upset when he couldn't get it back on.

Father asked for the toy, fixed the wheel, and returned it to Tomasito. The boy's face lit up and, tightly clutching the car, he ran excitedly from the room.

A short while later, Doña Juana entered with some other women. They carried platters filed with freshly cooked ears of corn, homemade cheese, and a dish of pink-skinned potatoes, lima beans, and garlic. Father gave a blessing for the food and another one for our host's home and family. After that, Doña Juana served us a rich vegetable soup. But neither she nor Don José sat down to eat with us.

Women started bringing in wooden chairs and placing them along the walls. A number of children sat there—Tomasito included, tightly holding his car. After we finished our meal and the plates had been cleared, the women and children moved to one side of the room, leaving empty chairs on the other. Then a group of elderly men followed Don José into the room in a solemn, almost ceremonial procession.

I could never have imagined what happened next...

*At Doña Juana's House*

# 10

## *A Message from the Elders*

We stood respectfully as the elders entered the room. They greeted us with dignified nods and went to sit along the wall opposite the women and children. Don José urged us to sit. He himself sat down and began speaking in a soft voice—so soft I had to listen really hard to hear.

"Don José, Doña Aida, señorita Yearim, señorita Tanis," he said, "My friends, welcome to my home and to the valley. I speak for the Council of Elders here in this room. It is not our way to make small talk when we have important things to say. So with your permission, I will speak.

"This world we live in is the causay pacha—the world of living energy," he said. "Everything is alive, everything speaks, and everything has something to give. But some energy is helpful and some is not. It is important to know the difference.

"The helpful energy is sami, the healthy energy of life, the light energy of healing. Sami is shared with us by the natural world: the sun, the wind, the rain, the rainbow, the moon, the stars, the mountains, the rivers, and the Earth with all its plants and animals. The unhelpful energy is hucha, a heavy energy generated by human fear, guilt, anxiety, and unresolved conflicts. Hucha contaminates a person's body and causes illness.

"Nature has the power to take heavy energy and turn it into light energy. To draw on that power you must be able to self-transform—a magical alchemy realized by self-healing.

"The Runa, as my people call ourselves, follow this practice. Each and every day we stand barefoot to watch the sun rise. To take in healing energy, we face the sun with our feet together and our arms wide open, inhaling deeply as we slowly draw our hands to our core. In doing this, we embrace sami, nature's healing energy, bringing it toward the belly to renew ourselves. We hold our breath for a while and then open our arms as we intone the word hucha—releasing all that is dense and heavy in our lives with our outgoing breath and expanding arms. We do this three times each morning. Then, still facing the sun, we chant a prayer. Seven times we repeat *Punchao chinam*—Let it dawn in our lives."

The process Don José described reminded me of a dome of protection, but I wondered if it had anything to do with my sash. So I asked.

"The tocapu on your sash says ayni. Ayni means reciprocal goodwill," he said. "Ayni is a good energy. You and your family put it into practice it by keeping a careful balance between getting and giving. Even without the sash, we can see the ayni in your poq'po."

Yaya asked, "What's a poq'po?"

"The poq'po is an energetic field around the body," Don José replied. "It's like a cocoon that protects your body and keeps you connected to life. Good energy called sami enters your body through your poq'po. Taking in sami and releasing hucha is how you cleanse the poq'po—something you may find useful in the days to come."

"Is a poq'po like an aura?" I asked.

"Yes, it is!" he answered. "Despite your youth, you are quite well educated."

"This incarnation may be young," said the tallest elder, "but if you consider prior incarnations, this young woman is the oldest person here."

Extending his arm toward the tall man, Don José said, "Esteemed guests, allow me to introduce Don Antonio Amaru, our curac acullec—what you might call a shaman. He is the ultimate authority for this Council of Elders.

"Each elder here comes from a different community, some quite far from the others," Don José explained. "We may live in rural villages scattered across the mountains, but we are not isolated and uninformed. The Earth speaks and keeps records of everything that happens.

"For instance," he said, "the Council meets several times a year in Ollantaytambo, but we never schedule our meetings ahead of time. We each learn from the natural world when something important or truly extraordinary is about to happen. The first alert comes from birdsongs and we confirm them with signs from the heavens and the Earth. Then we prepare and carry out the necessary actions. That is why we are here tonight."

Don José grew quiet. Then the shaman, Don Antonio, began to speak. "You are a remarkable family. We are honored by your presence," he said. "Once people adopt the practice of ayni, they share our way—the Runa way of life. Ayni is the key to appropriate human relations; and your family appears to practice it naturally and respectfully. Because of this you are now and always will be welcome among us.

"You are also exceptional," he added, "because those who brought you here and announced your presence to us were the Apus, the spirit guardians of the mountains."

Under her breath Yaya whispered, "The Elder from the Mountain!" I nodded.

"For centuries," Don Antonio explained, "we have kept alive the memory of magnificent sky beings who gave our ancestors great teachings about how to grow plants, how to domesticate animals, how to weave textiles, and how to work with stones—not simply with the physical properties of each but with their living essence.

"They taught us about the cycle of all things and promised to return at the change of times when we had evolved enough to overcome pain and suffering. We knew they would communicate with us through gentiles—outsiders from the city, people like you who would come to remind us of that promise and indicate that the change of times was imminent.

"We have been preparing all our lives for the return of those magnificent beings. Anyone who makes suitable preparations can channel, but you are uniquely qualified for contact with the celestials. This Council convened because you have that power."

Looking directly at me, Don Antonio said, "On behalf of the Council of Elders, I ask you to use your gift."

I nodded and was so full of emotion I didn't notice what Yaya or my parents were doing.

"We will meet again. Not here, but at Lake Huaypo," said Don Antonio. "The Piscorunas are sure to be there. If you have arrived, they will come. In three days we will have an appointment with the Piscorunas."

"What are Piscorunas?" I asked.

"Piscorunas are beings from another plane but they are also go-betweens," explained Don Antonio. "They don't easily fit into this-worldly categories, so it's hard to describe them. Some say they are bird-like creatures with human features. Some call them sky-people.

How they are described is not important. What matters is that by traveling between the stars and here, the Piscorunas unite heaven and Earth."

"Wow!" I exclaimed. "In a dream, the Elder from the Mountain spoke of a lake where large and unusual birds appear from time to time. Was she talking about Piscorunas?"

"That may be," Don Antonio replied. "Some say they soar like falcons."

Yaya's eyes met mine. She wanted to see the Piscorunas as much as I did. But our parents looked uneasy.

"What's this appointment?" Father asked uncertainly. "Why should we go to the lake?"

"Father," I said with as much calmness as I could manage, "I think Don Antonio is talking about beings like Ojito and other space-friends I've told you about."

"Am I to understand," Father said as he looked from me to Don José to Don Antonio, "that in three days we will have an encounter with extraterrestrials?"

There was a palpable and awkward silence in the room. The Elders looked at the ground as if to confirm Father's assumption.

I knew this was the message the Elder from the Mountain had promised. I just knew it! But Father looked so uncomfortable, I had to say something more. "Don Antonio," I began, "a luminous sphere I call Ojito has visited me for years. In dreams he has taken me in spaceships to other worlds where I met extraterrestrials, so I know they exist. I've even seen Ojito with wide-awake eyes. So has my whole family."

Addressing my parents, Don Antonio said, "Your daughter seems to have been your teacher in this regard. She and her friend Ojito have been preparing you."

To me he said, "You and many others will benefit from your experiences, both those in the past and those to come. Our people will benefit because of you. What occurs at the lake will rebuild the celestial bridge and reopen direct communication with our ancestors. For five hundred years we have been immersed in a terrible darkness set off by the brutal destruction of our way of life. For centuries there has been much sadness here, yet now a better time is at hand."

Don Antonio approached Yaya and me. "I will give each of you a special stone," he said. "They are cuyas, ritual stones that hold and transmit our mystical lineage. We ask you to present them to the

Piscorunas so they will know we have faithfully maintained the ancient knowledge."

He gave one stone to Yaya and one to me. White and egg-shaped, mine was remarkably warm.

"Don Antonio, why do you want my daughters to do this?" Mother asked.

"Because they are young women," he replied. "It is time for the magic of female energy to guide humanity. Women must lead humankind in renewing a respectful connection to Mother Earth. Your daughters have ancient, courageous spirits and in prior incarnations they developed strong and loving ties to this valley. Did they not bring you here?"

Content with his answer, Mother nodded.

"Prepare yourselves," advised Don Antonio. "We meet again at the lake."

Less hesitant that before, Father asked when.

"Go when your heart tells you to," Don José replied. "Pay attention to the area around your umbilicus—your center, where your inner sun resides. It will speak to you."

The elders rose and bade us farewell. They left one by one until only Don José, Doña Juana, Tomasito, and a man we didn't know remained. Doña Juana introduced us to Ernesto, her son and Tomasito's uncle. Ernesto offered to walk us back to our car, an offer we gratefully accepted.

While the narrow streets were extremely dark, the Milky Way flooded the heavens with light. The sky was so full of stars it looked white! Yaya asked for the Quechua name of the Milky Way and Ernesto said it was usually called Mayu—meaning River, though some people called it Ch'aska Mayu or Star River.

"In the valley," Ernesto continued, "what mapmakers call the Urubamba River is known as Huilkamayu or Sacred River. To my people it is a mirror that reflects Mayu, the celestial river."

"Astrologers in other cultures held a similar view," Father commented. "It can be summed up by the phrase *as above, so below*."

"That's how my people see things," replied Ernesto. "So did the Inca. Just before the Spanish invaded this valley, there were indications in the Mayu that the bridge to the land of the ancestors was about to be washed away. Then the Pizarros arrived and the balanced Inca way of life was destroyed."

We had been so busy stargazing that Yaya and I didn't notice how cold it was until we started to shiver. We were really glad when Mother pulled our jackets from her bag. And we were happy to give her the cuyas for safekeeping when she suggested it. Then Ernesto guided us back to our car through the empty streets.

On the drive to Urubamba, Yaya was the first to notice two bright lights moving slowly across the sky on a parallel course. Father stopped the car so we could observe how they crossed and crisscrossed the valley. They were up fairly high and Father remarked that they weren't behaving like satellites or airplanes. When the lights disappeared behind a mountain, there was an enormous flash.

Next morning we rose early to go to Machu Picchu, the so-called lost city of the Incas. We couldn't drive because the only way there was by train or by foot. Hiking the Inca Trail took four days, so we opted for the train. But first we had to take a bus to Ollantaytambo. From there we would take the train to Aguas Calientes, a small town at the base of Machu Picchu where we planned to spend two nights.

On the bus, Yaya and I sat together and went over all that had happened since we came to the valley. We were talking so fast and got so excited that Mother urged us to calm ourselves. We did our best to comply by whispering.

At the train station in Ollantaytambo we saw people waiting for the train and local merchants. Then Father spotted Doña Juana with Tomasito on her back. She came to greet us.

"Hola, Doña Juanita!" Mother said warmly. "How did you know we'd take this train?"

"A hunch," she said. "Tourists often visit Ollantaytambo the day before Machu Picchu."

Handing Mother a paper package tied with string, Doña Juana smiled and said, "Here are some refried beans and boiled corn for your trip."

After we thanked her, Doña Juana became serious. "Don José asked me to tell you that your poq'po not only protects you individually, it also protects your family. But to do that, the family must stay in harmony. Those who would harm humanity feed on the animosity, mistrust, and despair harbored in the hearts of people who have become estranged from their families."

The train's whistle blew as it pulled into the station. People began moving toward the tracks. Holding her ground against the pressing crowd, Doña Juana spoke with more urgency. "Don José said it was important to warn you that you will be targets for harmful energies from time to time. If you trust, you will be magically protected."

Wide-eyed and suddenly uneasy, Yaya and I just looked at each other.

Smiling, Doña Juana said, "Take good care of yourselves mamita, papito, and beautiful girls. Vayan con Dios!"

We boarded the train and took our seats. A few minutes later, the couplings clanked noisily, we lurched forward, and the train began to move. Through the window we saw Doña Juana waving. Tomasito waved his car in solidarity. We waved back.

*Overlooking Machu Picchu*

# 11

## *The Citadel of Machu Picchu*

On the way to Aguas Calientes we left the Sacred Valley and descended over 2,000 feet to a tropical region. The railroad followed the Urubamba and, since our seats were on that side of the train, we had a good view.

When not looking out the windows, Yaya and I tried to write in our diaries. We didn't write much but I noted one thing: although I'd been looking all over for my stone-friend, Ojito said the wall was in Cuzco. When I didn't find her there I began looking everywhere else. But if she were in Cuzco, I'd only find her there. So I decided to trust that I'd find her before we left.

Here and there we saw children waving or women walking beside the tracks, shawls laden with goods. From time to time, we saw Inca terraces and ruins far up the slopes.

The early morning chill gave way to balminess. We started seeing huge agaves as the foothills became increasingly more lush. After a while, the temperature rose even more and vegetation closed in on both sides. The river frothed with whitewater as the valley narrowed to a canyon.

The train went through a short tunnel and emerged at the ruins of Qente, meaning hummingbird. We had reached the high jungle and could see orchids, bromeliads, and huge trees dripping with Spanish moss. Though we were moving too fast to see their jeweled bodies, I imagined hummingbirds were feeding on the bright tropical flowers.

Mother opened Doña Juana's food, which was as good as it smelled. Mother hoped it would last us until dinner but said that if we got hungry we could grab a snack at the archeological park.

The number of rapids increased and, just above the water line, we could see where the river had cut through the granite base of the mountains. Finally, we spotted modern buildings and the train came to a stop. We had arrived at Aguas Calientes, a small tourist-based town.

After checking in at our hotel, we went to the bus station because the only way to reach Machu Picchu was by bus or by foot. From the station however, nothing suggested there was anything but jungle growth on the incredibly steep mountain before us.

The bus began going slowly upwards, moving back and forth on narrow switchbacks. The drop increased sharply as it rose, so the ride was like something from an adventure movie. At certain points I was certain we'd fall to our deaths, but we made it to the top and found that the line to enter the site was really long. People from all over the world were waiting to get in.

"Machu Picchu means Old Peak," Father explained as we waited in line. "Built around 1450 as Pachacuti's royal estate and abandoned a century later, this place survived for four hundred years without being looted or vandalized because neither the conquistadors nor the Spanish colonial rulers knew about it.

"This site was put on the map in 1911 by Hiram Bingham, an explorer from the United States," he said. "Two families were farming here when, guided by one of their boys, Bingham arrived. He described it as a citadel because the deep gorges and steep mountains around it provided superb natural defenses."

Once inside the park, we followed a path to the first lookout for a view of the canyon and the Urubamba River that snaked around the base of the mountain.

"All that the Inca valued came together in this sacred geography," Father observed. "It has the nurturing Earth below, their sacred river, life-sustaining springs, sightlines to their holy mountains, rainbow bridges to the three worlds, and the illuminating sky above."

"Was everything sacred to the Inca?" I asked.

"Just about," he replied. "They saw the world as alive and their duty was to acknowledge and honor its holiness. They made their buildings and terracing fit the environment out of respect for the natural world on which their lives depended."

The next lookout was the Watchman's Hut. Set on a ridge between two peaks, we saw a graceful village of stone houses and terraces surrounded by thousand-foot drops. It reminded me of the ruins above Pisac, but instead of sitting above a well-farmed valley, Machu Picchu was an orderly island in a sea of wilderness.

At the site's south end countless agricultural terraces curved sinuously down a long slope—and just then supported a small herd of llamas. At the north end was an urban area divided by a broad swath of grassy plazas on terraces of different levels. Because Machu Picchu's hundred and forty buildings had never been ransacked, we were seeing a royal Inca estate that, minus thatched roofs, was largely the way they made it.

We walked toward the urban sector and headed for the Sacred Plaza, a cluster of buildings around a small raised plaza that included the Temple of the Three Windows. The temple was a wayrona, a three-sided structure that opened onto the small plaza. Its windows overlooked the large terraced plazas below. The Main Temple nearby was another wayrona, outside of which was a large, kite-shaped rock embedded in the ground. Yaya asked Father what it was.

"It represents the constellation Katachillay or cross," he answered. "We know it as the Southern Cross. Often depicted as a chakana, Katachillay lies along the Milky Way and was extremely important in Inca astronomy."

We were drawn to the Chamber of Ornaments behind the Main Temple. In addition to niches, it had a long stone bench where we sat to rest. Father said it was a place to communicate with the gods so Yaya and I wanted to use the cuyas to meditate there. She and I held a cuya as we each faced a different niche, got comfortable, closed our eyes, and started chanting, Punchao chinam—Let it dawn in our lives.

By and by, I had a vision of ancient people, many of them women in tunics, participating in Earth–honoring ceremonies involving coca leaves and chicha beer. That vision faded and I found myself in a large cave full of niches like the ones we were facing. Suddenly the Elder from the Mountain appeared and said I was on a good road and would have important experiences before I went home. Then that vision faded.

When I opened my eyes, several tourists stood at the entrance or inside the room. Mother put the cuyas away and as we were leaving a young Brazilian man approached Yaya to ask where he could find a tour that did the sort of things we had been doing. His question took her by surprise. She said we were not a tour group— we were a family and nothing more.

Our next destination was a terraced pyramid. We climbed seventy-eight steps to the only intihuatana the Spanish hadn't damaged. Carved from the mountain itself, Machu Picchu's

Intihuatana was a gray granite sculpture about the size of a grand piano. Above several stepped levels was a trapezoidal post about two feet high with a slightly inclined rectangular top.

Using his hiking compass, Father showed us how the sides of the post were orientation devices. Each pointed to a cardinal direction where an important Apu stood: Salkantay was due south, Pumasillo due west, Huayna Picchu due north, and Waqaywillca due east.

"Those mountains were important for both solar and stellar readings," Father explained. "Every star in our southern sky changes position over the course of a year, so we have nothing as reliable as the North Star for orientation. But one star cluster is visible all year—Katachillay, the Southern Cross. So how would you find it given that nothing in the night sky is stationary?."

He paused to let us know that the question was for real. After a little while Yaya said, "I'd figure out where it was compared to something that didn't move and was easy to find."

"Precisely!" declared Father. "The Incas used the Apus, the most visible things around. They compared Katachillay's sky path to different Apus and discovered that it rises to the east and sets to the west of Salkantay—Indomitable Peak, the tallest mountain in the region. One side of this intihuatana post points due south to Salkantay. Using it to find Katachillay, astronomers could then use Katachillay to locate other stars or constellations."

"I didn't know intihuatanas had anything to do with stars," Yaya said.

"Stars played a vital role in Inca astronomy—but so did the sun. Yancas, as Inca astronomers were called, would read the sun's position to learn when rituals should be held."

"Why is it called the sun's hitching post?" Yaya asked.

"Bingham may have made up the name by combining two Quechua words—inti meaning sun and huatana meaning to tie. A century ago people didn't know how the Inca read the heavens, so that seemed to describe its function," Father explained. "In fact, it's a complex instrument for monitoring the cyclical movement of many heavenly bodies.

"Even so, this one shows why the name stuck. It marks the March and September equinoxes in two different ways. First, on the morning of the equinox, yancas would see the sun rise directly behind Waqaywillca's highest peak, due east of the post. The second reading confirmed the first. At noon on the equinox, the sun stands directly above the post. So for a short period when the sun stops moving, the post has no shadow. It was during that magical period when the sun did not move that it seemed to be tied or hitched to the post."

Descending from the pyramid, we made our way to the terraces that spanned the urban sector and sat on the grass to rest. This was the plaza where public rituals had been held. In looking around, the Temple of the Three Windows caught my eye. Its large windows and great polygonal ashlars were especially striking from below. When I told Father that the temple made me think of the three caves in the Ayar brothers' legend, he said that's probably what it was meant to do.

From there we headed to the Sacred Rock at the edge of the northern abyss. Flanked by two wayronas and enshrined within a low stone wall, it was a huge gray granite boulder twenty-five feet long and ten feet high. Its outline mirrored the shape of Yanantin, the mountain behind it.

"Yanantin is more than a word in Quechua. It is a major concept that represents the harmonious relationship between opposites—male and female, light and dark, right and left," Father said. "Central to the Inca worldview, Yanantin describes a dualistic yet balanced marriage of two distinct equals. The Sacred Rock represents the Inca idea of integration."

"Does yanantin have anything to do with *as above, so below*?" Yaya asked.

"Yes," he replied, "They both involve complementary relationships."

"What about yin-yang?" I asked.

"It's very much like the yin-yang concept," said Father, smiling at both of us.

During the afternoon we explored workers' dwellings, caves, and rooms with powerful boulders. Then we entered the Temple of the Condor, a bird that embodies the spirit of the Apus. Set in the ground within its walls was a flat, triangular rock on which stonemasons had etched the outline of a condor's head. Two huge, jagged rocks were positioned above it in a dramatic V-shape that resembled condor wings—either just opening to take flight or just closing to land.

Father said some people thought the flat rock had been an altar for llama sacrifices. I asked why.

"According to some stories, llamas accompanied the Ayars when they emerged from the cave at Pacaritampu," he replied.

"Essential to survival in the high mountains, llamas were highly valued as service animals that could carry loads up steep slopes and provide wool for clothes."

"If they liked llamas so much," Yaya asked, "why did they sacrifice them?"

"Old religions weren't easy on their followers," Father explained. "Just as the God of the Israelites asked Abraham to sacrifice what he most valued—a beloved son, the Inca believed they had to offer their gods what they valued most. Otherwise it wouldn't have been a sacrifice."

Walking uphill we reached the Temple of the Sun—also called the Tower, a two-story structure with the finest stonework in Machu Picchu. Grafted onto a natural outcrop that serves as its foundation, the turret has a curved wall that enshrines a huge boulder called a sunstone.

As Father demonstrated, platforms and notches in the stone aligned with windows on the wall. "At the December solstice, sunlight comes through the southeast window and touches a precise point on the stone," he said. "While the northeast window is a marker for the June solstice, it also frames the return of Qollqa in early June. We know Qollqa as the Pleiades star cluster, but in Quechua it means storehouse—a granary like those we saw from afar at Ollantaytambo.

"Yancas knew that the celestial atmosphere was linked to the Earth's climate, so how Qollqa looked when it reappeared in June gave them important information. If the cluster looked large and bright, they knew rainfall would be normal. If it appeared small and dim, the valley would experience the extreme weather pattern modern scientists call El Niño. "When Qollqa was hard to see, it meant there'd be little rain and corn crops would require extra irrigation."

Underneath the sunstone was a cave that had been worked by stonemasons until the natural and handmade blended into a single entity. The cave's wall had been carved into four steps that went nowhere, like a blind-door. Father said the cave had been a mausoleum for royal mummies. The steps marked a transition between worlds—probably to and from the realm of the ancestors.

The Royal Palace was just beyond the Temple of the Sun, but it was more than I could take in. By then I had walked so much my feet hurt. It wasn't just me—we were all tired. So we decided to go back to Aguas Calientes and return the next day to hike up Huayna Picchu.

The bus ride down was more hair-raising than the ride up but we reached the town in one piece, rested for a while at our hotel, and had a nice dinner in a restaurant on the rushing river. Though it rained later that night, the sky was clear and full of stars when we were out.

While Yaya and I were getting ready for bed, we talked about our experiences with the cuyas. She had seen a ñusta or Inca priestess walk toward the building we were in. The ñusta sat facing a niche and began praying for the protection of the citadel, the king, the queen, and the empire.

I told Yaya about my experience and she just nodded.

That night I dreamt about the Elder and the ñustas—but Yaya and I were also ñustas.

*Yaya and John on Huayna Picchu*

# 12

## A Bird's-Eye View

Aguas Calientes was named for its hot springs, so we got up very early to enjoy them. The springs were on one end of town, just beyond the built-up area, and it wasn't a far walk. But getting there was a bit dicey because it was still quite dark in the valley.

Atop a hill we found several geothermally heated pools, some warmer than others. We chose a very warm one that was fed directly from deep within the mountain. Its healing liquid was rich in minerals that gave it a strong and unpleasant odor that we tried our best to ignore.

As the first rays of sun appeared, we entered the pool and stayed for a long time, soaking, paddling around, and just floating. We had the place all to ourselves, since no one else had ventured there so early in the day.

When Mother became dizzy, Father helped her out of the pool. Then we all got dressed and headed slowly back to our hotel, allowing the heat and the minerals to work on our bodies. My legs felt rubbery-loose, an odd but good feeling.

After showering and having a quick breakfast, we took the bus to Machu Picchu and arrived much earlier than the day before. Still damp from the morning mist, the ruins looked magical. Dewdrops dazzled like diamonds in the sunlight. We peered into the gorge and saw wispy clouds clinging to treetops below the sun's reach. Just above them was a rainbow.

Yaya and I felt blessed by the rainbow, so we each made a wish. I wished to find my stone-friend before I went home. I kept it a secret so it would come true. Yaya kept hers a secret too.

We admired the apparition until it started evaporating. Before it completely vanished, Father asked what we saw when we looked at the rainbow.

"Magical light of different colors," I replied.

"An arc," Yaya added.

"To us a rainbow is a half circle of colored light," Father said. "To the Inca it was a full circle, only half of which was visible. The other half went underground to complete the circle."

"Is that how rainbows bridge the worlds—or whatever you said yesterday?" Yaya asked.

"Yes," he replied. "A rainbow begins on the ground, bends through the plane of this-world to the sky, and touches ground again where, in the Inca view, it goes underground. In so doing, the rainbow connects the three worlds—Ukju Pacha, Kay Pacha, and Hanan Pacha."

"That's like what Ernesto said about the Milky Way and the Urubamba River," Yaya remarked. "The Mayu is above, the Huilkamayu is below."

"Exactly!" said Father. "As above, so below."

We headed to the wayronas at the entrance to Huayna Picchu—Old Peak. Once there, however, mother said she didn't feel up to the climb and preferred to stay below rather than hold us up. Father respected her decision and they agreed to rendezvous at the wayrona in three hours.

Though wary of the climb, I was willing to do it. But I didn't want Mother to be left alone so I decided to stay with her. Protesting that she'd be fine and I shouldn't miss the climb, Mother only let me stay when it became clear that I intended to do just that.

Father and Yaya signed in at the ranger's station, a checkpoint where hikers must register by name, age, nationality, time of entry, and estimated time of exit. This was a safety precaution in case someone went missing, which has happened.

As Yaya explained to me later, the beginning of the hike was rather easy. When the path went dangerously close to the abyss, there were thick cables to hold onto. In other places, steps had been cut into the mountain. The hike took about an hour and got harder the longer they climbed, perhaps because of the altitude. The zigzagging path offered splendid views and places to rest along the way.

Near the summit, steps led through a serpentine cave to the very top. Once there, Father sat down to rest, catch his breath, and admire the panorama. Yaya stood exultant, turning full circle to take it all in. She said the entirety of Machu Picchu resembled a condor in flight. Finally sitting, she dangled her legs over the abyss, while father took photos. Then a young man approached her.

"Weren't you and your family in Ollantaytambo a few days ago?" he asked in an unusual accent.

"Yes, we were."

"My name is John," the young man said, introducing himself in a friendly way. "By some coincidence, we've been in the same places at the same time. I watched your family put your hands on the temple wall at Ollantaytambo and wanted to learn why."

Pleased by his manner, Yaya introduced herself and said, "We touched the wall because each stone has a particular energy. Feeling the stones is a way to connect with the story of the place."

"Where did you learn that?" he asked.

"An extraterrestrial taught my sister and she taught my parents and me."

"Your parents had contact with ETs?" John exclaimed with wide eyes.

"Not directly, but they saw things that confirm what my sister says. They're open to such things, so we all talk about it. In fact, our whole family has been invited to meet some extraterrestrials the highlanders call Piscorunas."

"Really?" said John. "May I come?"

"Probably not," she replied. "I think you have to be invited by the Elders."

"Could you ask them to invite me? I really want to come."

"Maybe I shouldn't have mentioned it because it's not about what you or I want," she said kindly. "If ETs want to contact you, they'll find you. But it's good to be prepared."

"How can I do that?" he asked.

"Well, I think attitude's the biggest thing," she explained. "You don't have to worry so much about how to prepare, if you just stay open. When people harden their hearts or lose emotional balance, their energy unravels from their family and friends. Then they're vulnerable to dark shadows."

"What are dark shadows?" John asked.

"Dark shadows come from destructive emotions. Feelings like envy, blame, and resentment can build up into an evil force that overtakes a person's thoughts and feelings. But dark energy is so dense that in the long run it actually sinks of its own weight. When that happens it nurtures goodness—the way compost helps plants grow."

Just then John's parents called him in English, saying they were getting ready to leave.

"I wonder if I'll see you again," he mused. "I'd like to."

"Who knows?" Yaya replied with a wistful shrug. "It's been a pleasure talking with you."

John gently touched Yaya's hand, which made her blush. Then he walked away. Yaya thought he was very nice. And handsome too.

While Father and Yaya were starting their ascent of Huayna Picchu, Mother and I communed with the Sacred Rock. We put our hands and foreheads on the giant stone and followed what, by then, was our usual deep breathing process. We spent quite some time with the magnificent stone, and thanked it when we left to sit in the wayrona and share our experiences.

The rock communicated to me only in images for which I don't even have words. It had something to do with centers or being centered. The feeling I got reminded me of the time I was in a small boat on choppy waters. Trying to keep my balance as the boat rocked back and forth was not unpleasant, but it made me pay attention to everything.

Mother experienced a deep grounding and an almost musical sense of harmony. "If I were a composer—a really good composer," she said, "I might try to express it in music."

Neither of us wanted to do much climbing, so we went to the main square and watched the llamas grazing. Then we walked to the ritual fountains near the Royal Palace. The artfully connected cascades and the sound of running water were so pleasant that we lingered there.

Later, on our way to the palace, we passed the Temple of the Sun and something made me want to revisit it. Mother agreed to meditate there with me so we climbed to its upper landing and sat facing the sunstone with our backs to a wall.

After gazing at it for a while with eyes half-open and half-closed, Mother seemed to fall asleep. I closed my eyes and inhaled deeply, focusing on my breath the way Ojito had taught me. Sitting in the warm sun, I imagined I was lying on a beach, with waves rhythmically washing over my legs. I began feeling lighter and lighter, floating just like I did in the hot springs that morning. Then I felt my astral body rise.

From above I could see myself sitting on the landing with Mother napping next to me. When I looked around I saw the whole of Machu Picchu. I had an extraordinary bird's-eye view of it and everything around it. I felt that I was flying, actually rising.

A condor flew near me. I got really excited and then noticed a white-spot on its chest, which was unusual, since condors have dark breast feathers. Suddenly my body merged with his: I saw through his eyes, breathed with his lungs, and felt the push of air against his wings. Rising thermals were lifting and holding us aloft. We soared above Huayna Picchu, where I saw Yaya and Father. Then the condor banked and we practically slid along an air current, taking in the sky above, the green mountains around, and the silver-white river below.

Some time later, my awareness was drawn to the Temple of the Sun. I saw it as a shining tower of granite—but it was also alive. It sprouted like a tree from the very ground beneath it. Strong roots extended down from the cave into the mountain below. A rainbow curved around the sunstone and from it rays of light spread like branches into the sky.

I heard a voice inside my head say, "This magical ladder unites the Ukju Pacha and the Hanan Pacha by means of the Kay Pacha." And I could see how its very structure and the intention with which it had been built connected the three worlds.

Then, as if from far away, I heard Mother calling my name. She called and called, very gently, until I opened my eyes—reluctantly because I hadn't wanted my journey to end.

Mother said she had dozed off and awoke to find me in a sort of trance. I explained what happened so she told me to rest until I felt strong enough to get up and helped me stand when I did. She made me drink some water and eat some dried fruit. Then we descended to the terrace-path that led to the main plaza and headed toward Huayna Picchu. We were late for our rendezvous at the Sacred Rock.

It so happened that Father and Yaya started looking for us when they didn't find us at the wayrona. As they approached the main plaza, Yaya spotted us in the distance. By the time they reached us, I felt well grounded. Mother explained what had occurred and Father said it would do me good to walk for a bit so we made our way to the exit.

We took the bus back to Aguas Calientes, had lunch, and caught the afternoon train as planned. Once aboard and in our seats, we all fell asleep. Fortunately Father woke up before we reached Ollantaytambo, otherwise we might have gone all the way to Cuzco.

A minibus driver from the Urubamba hotel met us at the station. Friendly and quite talkative, he introduced himself as Alberto and asked how our trip had gone. After Father said it went very well, the driver related the news.

"I don't know if you follow such things but a Cuzco newspaper reported that for the past two nights tourists have seen strange lights around Lake Huaypo. There have been many reports of such things in that area over the years," Alberto said.

"What time were the lights seen?" Father asked. "And how did people describe them?"

"The article said that when first seen on the horizon the lights were white and strong, then they separated into different colors—some yellow and gold, others red and blue. Some people believe it was an airplane crash, but that couldn't have happened two nights in a row," the driver mused.

"So it happened at night?" Father inquired, trying to clarify what had happened.

"Around seven or eight at night. But I saw something very odd early this morning after leaving Cuzco. Though it was still dark, I detoured to check out Lake Huaypo on my way here and you won't believe what I saw! I wish I'd had a camera," said the driver.

"What did you see?" asked Father.

"I saw a group of highlanders making offerings to the lake. I watched them closely for some time before I saw a huge bird or something like that from the corner of my eye. When I turned to look at it directly, it was gone. But I did see it—I swear! And I had not been drinking," exclaimed Alberto.

"I've heard of such things," said Father.

"It gave me quite a jolt," Alberto exclaimed. "An odd thing, no?"

"Quite so," Father replied.

Alberto and Father discussed various topics all the way back to the hotel. As they did, Yaya and I told Mother and each other what we had done while we were apart.

That night we stayed at the hotel in Urubamba. The next day we were to meet the Piscorunas.

*Old Woman with Firewood at Chinchero*

# 13

## *Sojourn at Chinchero*

After five days of intense sightseeing, we slept in. Following breakfast we got ready to go to Chinchero, which is on a high plateau about 12,400 feet above sea level—higher than any place we'd been so far. We planned to explore the town and its ruins, have lunch, and head to Lake Huaypo when the time seemed right.

Saying an invocation before we left, we envisioned a white light descending over us as well as the car, forming a protective dome. Then we set off. The trip was only twelve miles and Father figured it would take half an hour. But as soon as we crossed the Urubamba River and began ascending a winding mountain road, Mother said she had a bad feeling.

Ten minutes later, a public bus came hurtling towards us at considerable speed. It swerved from one side of the road to the other, apparently out of control, and barely missed us before crashing into a wall. Once the bus stopped moving, Father pulled to the side of the road. We stayed in the car while he went to see if he could be of any help.

Police and firemen arrived a while later. There were no mobile phones in rural areas then, so I'm not sure how they found out. Emergency responders from Urubamba offered first-aid. The side of the bus was so badly crushed that passengers had to exit through the rear. Most of them were scared and banged up, but not too seriously.

We were all right so we continued on to Chinchero. Being on a spiritual path does not prevent bad things from happening, but this near miss confirmed our family's sense that protection and support is often granted when you ask for it with faith.

Nevertheless, following the accident, Father drove with noticeable care. As he did, we saw a gently rolling landscape with amazing mountain views, including one of the snow-capped Chicon—Valiant Man. And Father told us about Chinchero.

For starters its name means place of the rainbows. Located in a rich agricultural area on a plateau above the Sacred Valley, Chinchero is the mythic birthplace of the rainbow.

Built in 1480 by the Inca king Túpac Yupanqui, the town is famous for preserving its pre-Hispanic traditions and is one of the few that still has an ayllu community structure. A system that preceded the Incas, the ayllu is a form of government made up of members of an extended family that collectively owns the land its people farm. Each ayllu has a leader who is like a mayor, and each usually has its own hauca—a site-specific deity embodied in a boulder, a spring, or a nearby mountain. Chinchero has twelve ayllu communities.

Mother said Chinchero also has a big market, less touristy than Pisac, where they still use barter as a way of doing business. Tuesday was a market day and we'd be able to see it for ourselves. Mother also said the town was renowned for its weaving and she wanted to check out the cooperatives that use traditional weaving methods.

Set on a slope, the town extends up from the old Inca plaza. Father parked as close as he could and we walked the rest of the way. The plaza was full of vendors and shoppers, but there were fewer tourists than at Pisac. We meandered through the lively market, enjoying the colorful outfits of the women and watching a couple of barters. Since the transactions were in Quechua, we could only observe, but it was fun to watch.

We eventually came to a long stone wall that enclosed a platform around a colonial church famous for its interior frescoes. But it wasn't open so all we saw was how, in a fusion of cultures, the Catholic church had incorporated the stone wall from the Inca palace.

We'd seen other signs of that fusion as we walked to the square: most of the town's houses had terracotta roofs topped by a crucifix and a pair of bulls. The cross is a sign of Catholic devotion, while the bulls honor Pachamama and displaying them is an Earth-honoring prayer to bring prosperity, happiness, and fertility to the household.

Held in place by extensive Inca terracing, the terrain dropped away from two sides of the plaza. One area had an amphitheater with shrines dedicated to huacas, local deities or mythic ancestors, and we headed toward a huge rock with unusual carvings. On the way there, Yaya and I saw an old woman carrying an enormous bundle of wood in a shawl across her back. In her hands, she was spinning wool into yarn. She seemed totally at ease, walking with a small dog at her side.

My parents nodded hello and she smiled back. Yaya and I did the same as we were about to climb onto the huaca. But instead of smiling and going on her way, she approached us and said, "mamita! What are you doing?"

"We're exploring this stone, Señora," Yaya replied.

The old woman's question seemed like a warning, so I was glad she saw us before we got on the huaca or it would have been embarrassing. In looking at her, I wondered about the load she was carrying. I asked, "Señora, is your bundle heavy?"

"It would be a heavier burden to not carry it, my beauty!" she said. "It is cold in these mountains. This firewood will allow my family to heat our home and cook our food. It seemed heavy when I started out, but the closer I get to home the less it weighs.

"Burdens become problems when they are carried with resentment," she continued. "I carry this firewood with love and doing it for my family makes the task less difficult. Despite my age, I am strong. But I have a little trick to avoid thinking about the weight of the wood—I focus on the yarn as I spin it. The less I think about the burden of the wood, the less it weighs."

With that the old woman nodded and went on her way, walking amazingly fast.

We returned to the plaza and wandered from merchant to merchant, examining all their offerings. Produce vendors had various types of potatoes and several types of beans including lima beans and tarwi, sometimes called the Andean soybean. And they were selling maize in three forms: dried on the cob, separated into dried kernels, and ground into flour for making tortillas and tamales. There were also root vegetables such as onions and sweet potatoes, green vegetables, various fruits, and different kinds of cheese. We even saw people selling medicinal herbs.

Mother finally found women from the weaving cooperative who directed us to their workshop. The weavings they made were remarkable. Their designs and colors were subtle but more alive than any weavings we had seen thus far. When Mother commented on that, one of the women said the patterns were ancient traditional designs and the colors came from natural dyes.

She explained that the women in her cooperative use only local plants, minerals, and insects. Chamomile, for instance, makes wool yellow. Different plants, such as chilca or ragwort, make wool green. The shrub known as tara and blue colpa, an iron sulphate, turn wool blue. Reds come from the female cochineal beetle, a tiny insect found on the prickly pear cactus. And the particular color of red—ranging from scarlet to orange, from purple to pink—depends on how much dye is used, how long the wool stays immersed, and whether lemon or salt is added to the dye-water to alter its pH level.

Mother was so impressed by the weavings that she bought a few shawls as gifts. She also bought Yaya and me each a rainbow-colored chullo, the high Andes knitted caps with earflaps. Since she didn't have anything to trade, mother used cash. But that's what the women seemed to expect from a tourist.

Later we bought tamales, fruit, and bottled water from market vendors and Mother laid plastic sheets on some grass beyond the plaza. After a nice picnic lunch, we all lay down for a siesta.

Father woke us. He said something had awakened him—possibly the cold. It had gotten quite cool. Chinchero is 1,300 feet higher than Cuzco, so it gets chilly in the afternoon.

We went to the car to get our jackets. Yaya and I even put on our chullos, which were very warm. Then we got into the car and headed for Lake Huaypo. None of us raised the question of what would happen once we got there, but then none of us—including Father—really knew what to expect.

*Elder Wearing Poncho and Chullo*

# 14

## *Appointment with the Piscournas*

Initially Father drove back on the same highway we took to Chinchero. Halfway to Urubamba, he turned left onto a dirt road that ran between fields of potatoes and olluco, a high Andes root vegetable similar to the potato.

After a while we could see the lake in the distance. When the road dipped, the lake disappeared but came into view again at the next rise. The road curved around the long, western edge of the lake, so we got to see it from several angles before we stopped at its southern end. It was almost six o'clock and the sky was still light.

The lake was beautiful but so isolated it felt a bit otherworldly. With no wind, the glassy water reflected the sky and distant mountains like a mirror. We were actually comforted when we spotted a white heron and heard other birds call from the marsh grass along the shore.

Mother took out a thermos of coca tea and Father spread plastic sheets for us to sit on. When we finished the tea, we found comfortable meditation positions facing the lake and, with closed eyes, reverently chanted Don José's door-opening mantra, Punchao chinam.

We must have chanted for a long time because when Mother urged us to open our eyes, it was dark. We had an unobstructed view of the Milky Way and marveled at the sky until Father noticed a procession of candles heading our way.

Assuming it was the Elders, he blinked his flashlight to let them know where we were. It took a while, but the candles eventually reached us. Led by Ollantaytambo's Elders, the procession included family members and others I did not recognize. The men wore ponchos and chullos, while the women had on their best traditional outfits.

"Please accept our apologies," said Don José. "We did not mean to disturb you."

"No problem, Don José. We're glad to see you," Mother replied with relief.

"It is time," Don Antonio announced in a ceremonial tone.

There by the side of the lake the procession encircled us. Don José, Doña Juana, and Don Antonio joined us in the center. They remained standing as everyone else sat on the ground. Don José and Doña Juana acted as ceremonial helpers, bringing Don Antonio some chicha de jora, coca leaves, and an incense burner like you see in church. Don Antonio prayed aloud in Quechua, making offerings of chicha, coca, and incense to Mother Earth.

As soon as he made the offerings, Don Antonio asked us to stand. Doña Juana smudged us by moving the censor and fanning the incense smoke so it moved over our heads, our hearts, and our bodies, cleansing us of hucha or heavy energies.

Don Antonio asked Mother for the cuyas, which she removed from her bag. He held one cuya in each hand as Doña Juana smudged them, after which Don Antonio showed them to everyone gathered there. Then he stood before Yaya and me. Extending a stone to each of us, he said, "Lovely young women, will you now offer our lineage to the Piscorunas?"

Once we accepted the cuyas, the stars in the sky started moving and bright lights on the horizon shot sideways then split into multiple lights like fireworks. Laughing and commenting, the highlanders were enjoying the spectacle. I simply watched, overcome by an intensely peaceful feeling.

Some of the lights glided toward the lake. They hovered above the water and, when they got near us, shot into the sky at great speed. After a long period of silence, the lake began to glow. I heard a strange hum that increased until it sounded like a stampede of horses.

Those sitting nearest the shore got startled and shrank back as the water's surface began to curve up and glow like the moon. Suddenly there were bursts of light and the center of the lake became so bright it blinded me temporarily. When I could see again, a disk-like shape hovered above the water. The hoof beats subsided and the humming diminished to a distant drone.

A hatch on top of the disk opened and a pair of two-legged light beings emerged. They reminded me of light beings from

Morlen—what we call Ganymede, a large moon that orbits Jupiter—where Ojito comes from and I'd gone on astral journeys. I wondered if Ojito was with them...

At that moment, the highlanders welcomed their ancient teachers. "Huari, Huari, Huari, Hauri," they chanted rhythmically.

A broad beam of light spread slowly from disk to shore, forming a luminescent bridge they glided across. As they drew near, the highlanders began a heart-opening chant, "Piscoruna... Piscoruna... Piscoruna..."

So luminous they dazzled my eyes, the beings appeared almost human. Though similar, one looked male, the other female. Both had triangular faces and shaggy, flame-like hair of a silvery blue. They also had almond shaped cat's eyes in a light amber color.

When the Piscorunas were about ten feet away from us they stopped. As the cuya grew hot in my hand and began to glow, I heard them speak telepathically. With one voice they said, "We are messengers from Morlen and we greet you! What do you hold in your hands?"

"We hold special stones that contain the mystical lineage of the Elders—all they learned, to whom they transmitted their wisdom teachings, and from whom they originally received their knowledge," I answered.

"Through us the Elders offer these cuyas to demonstrate how faithfully your teachings have been preserved and passed down through the centuries," Yaya added.

"We accept these offerings," they replied. "Place the cuya you hold against your forehead so we can read all that is registered within and also share its information with you."

When I touched the glowing stone to my forehead, my head felt like it cracked open. Images flooded in along with every emotion possible. I saw that space was full of holes—like Swiss cheese. On the cosmic highway, each was a portal or exit to a different space-time.

I also saw how human spiritual growth and the evolution of extraterrestrials were interwoven—something that began sixty-five million years ago when Earth was devastated by meteors. To prevent its complete annihilation, extraterrestrial engineers known as Experimenters traveled back through space-time by means of star gates. To do this, they created an alternate Earth-time that was incompatible with the real time of the universe. But it worked and the Earth was saved.

The inter-dimensional portal through which the Experimenters came to Earth was also their route home, provided they left within a given period of time. But they didn't. They delayed leaving and the portal they created opened other portals with parallel realities. So the Experimenters didn't know which was the route home and got stuck here on Earth.

To get out, they constructed twelve disks of a translucent gold that were positioned around the planet. When connected to a thirteenth disk and properly activated, those disks could open a portal that would let them go home. The disks would also align planet Earth with a wormhole through which it could pass into the real time of the universe.

But there were problems. While the Experimenters were highly evolved in most respects, they lacked emotions and emotions were essential for activating the disks. Moreover, those activating the disks had to be able to access higher spiritual realms, a capacity few if any humans possessed at the time. So the extraterrestrials developed a cosmic plan to nurture a civilization of loving humans who could access higher spiritual realms and teach them how to love.

As part of this plan, extraterrestrials from beyond Earth transported humans to other worlds to be educated. Manco Cápac and Mama Ocllo, founders of the Inca lineage, were instructed in that way and then returned to Earth to share their knowledge.

According to the cosmic plan, to be truly human is to love— an emotion expressed by giving and sharing with fellow humans. The plan did not go smoothly, however, because extraterrestrials did not anticipate how volatile human emotions could be.

Successive waves of extraterrestrials came to Earth to aid the Experimenters. But things went from bad to worse and conflict arose among the ETs. Eventually thirty-two mentors of light from different worlds, a community of benevolent extraterrestrials known as the Great White Brotherhood, came to Earth and settled in the Gobi Desert. Their mission was to correct the errors that had been made, restrict the participation of renegade ETs, and build the thirteenth golden disk—the matrix that would unite all the others.

Now the Earth is coming to the end of a cycle. The planet has reached a major turning point and is undergoing changes that will initiate a new reality. Hand in hand with those changes, many humans have developed the awareness and spiritual maturity to access that new reality. By working with the transformational cosmic energies now available, those people can foster a collective awakening for all humanity.

The inflow of information slowed as I recognized the limits of our concept of time as linear and sequential. Once our planet goes through the wormhole, Earth's alternative time will synchronize with and merge into the real time of the universe—the fourth dimension. It will be obvious then that not only does time move in a spiral but also there are concurrently overlapping space-times within the greater space-time of the universe.

The transmission ended and our cuyas glowed even more intensely. They rose above our heads and flew to the hands of their keeper, the shaman, Don Antonio.

Speaking with one voice, the Piscorunas said, "The time shift is imminent. There is much at stake—especially in your global year 2012 and after. As Earth-time and all that goes with it changes, humans must transform to survive. All conditions are now in place to activate the thirteenth disk and open the portal to a new era."

"It must be initiated by female energy," announced the female. "None can do this better than you young women, star children who have come to Earth to usher in this era."

"How can we do that?" asked Yaya, ready to accept the challenge.

"Use your inner power," the female replied. "That power manifests through mind and word. The mind is will and consciousness. Knowing you can do it and wanting to do it are empowered by the intentional vibration of sound—the word, spoken or chanted.

"The future of the world is in human hands," she continued. "To successfully transition to the new era, humans must master their emotions and grow spiritually—and we are watching to see how this unfolds."

"Timing is critical," cautioned the male. "Because the cosmic shift has begun, the Dark Shadow is breeding chaos and using increasingly drastic measures to keep humans ignorant of their true powers. Down through the ages the Dark Shadow has felt so threatened by the human capacity that it infiltrated seats of power, from religious authorities to governments, in order to restrict and negate people's awareness of their own potential."

Speaking jointly again, they counseled, "Remember that for every force there is an equal and opposite force. Even the darkest of forces is not superior to its complement or counterpart, so trust in the possibility of creating a proper balance by keeping a positive attitude. As events happen, you will know what to do. Trust that a higher power—one beyond all comprehension—is there for you and let your heart guide you. Now go in peace!"

The two beings glided backwards. As they receded, I became aware that the highlanders were still chanting, "Piscoruna… Piscoruna…." The beings entered their spaceship and there was an intense vibration. I again heard the thunderous sound of running horses. Then the luminous disk submerged, leaving a profound stillness. The highlanders stopped chanting and all I heard for minutes on end was my own breathing and the beating of my heart.

A wind riffled the surface of the lake. It felt like a spell had been broken.

I looked at Yaya. She was radiant, beautiful. Our parents seemed dazed. Then the highlanders surrounded us, expressing their gratitude. Smiling, Doña Juana hugged us both and said, "Go with God, my blessed ones."

Don Antonio formally thanked Yaya and me and gave us each a small bundle of ceremonial cornmeal with a round, cat-eyed face on its wrapping. We thanked him for the gifts and watched the procession depart. The sight of the group's candles snaking along the road was unforgettable.

Finally by ourselves, we turned to our parents. In the midst of bidding farewell to everyone else, we'd forgotten how subdued they were. Yaya suggested they might be in a trance like when I do an astral journey. Very gently, I called to Mother while Yaya called to Father. We stroked their palms as we called their names.

After awhile, Father came out of his stupor. "What a disappointment!" he said. "I never expected that nothing would happen!"

"How can you say that?" Yaya asked. "We met with two Piscorunas!"

Seconds later Mother shivered, looked around, and said, "I'm surprised the Elders never came."

I told her the Elders had come with a whole bunch of people, but she was unconvinced.

"Girls, that's enough!" Father declared. "I'm too tired for games."

Turning to Mother, he said, "Did you see anything?"

"No... but my thinking is fuzzy," she admitted.

"I think the altitude is getting to us," Father exclaimed. "Let's go back to Cuzco."

Yaya and I looked at each other. We were speechless. I wondered how they could have sat through the whole spectacle without remembering any of it.

Neither of us said any more. Nor did we insist that anything had occurred. Instead, we helped gather our stuff and headed for the car. Before I got in, however, I turned to look at the lake. I wanted to remember how it looked under the stars for the rest of my life.

*Piscorunas Appear at Lake Huaypo*

# 15

## *Inside the Golden Courtyard*

We slept rather late because Father got lost and didn't reach the hotel until nearly eleven. When we finally roused ourselves, we had breakfast at the hotel. I felt like I hadn't eaten in weeks. In fact, we were all hungry. The amount of food we ate astonished the waiter. We devoured fruit, toast, and scrambled eggs like piranhas.

During breakfast, Yaya and I tried to find out if our parents remembered anything from the lake. Except for admitting it was unusual for him to get lost in Cuzco, Father thought nothing had happened. So did Mother.

Yaya and I talked things over as we brushed our teeth after breakfast. Maybe holding the cuyas allowed us to recall the experience so we could tell others. Aside from their amnesia about events at the lake, our parents seemed quite normal. So we decided to watch and wait: why they couldn't recall anything would either reveal itself or remain a mystery. The problem was we couldn't talk with them about the Piscorunas' message. Regarding that we were on our own.

By returning to Cuzco, we had completed a circle and this was the last day of our journey. We were leaving in the afternoon, so our only plan was to visit the Coricancha, the principal Inca temple, which we could reach by foot from our hotel.

As we walked, Father reminded us that Cuzco means navel of the world. "That's more than a metaphor," he explained. "The Inca saw Cuzco as the place where the Earth was linked to the heavens. An unborn child is linked to its mother by an umbilical cord; after birth, the navel shows where the link was and serves as an energy conduit. Cuzco was the energy center of the Inca world—the place where celestial order and authority were transmitted to Inca rulers.

"One Inca myth begins when the sun god saw that the people of Earth were living like wild beasts. People lived without houses or cities, without laws or rituals to honor him, and without cultivating the land or wearing clothes. Seeing this, Inti took pity on them and sent Manco Cápac and Mama Ocllo, his son and daughter by the Moon, to teach people how to be civilized, how to build, how to weave, how to farm, and how to raise animals.

"Inti transported his children to Lake Titicaca, gave them a golden staff, and bade them find good farmland. He said they would know the right place when the golden rod sank into the ground with a single thrust. The children of the sun left the lake and walked north. As they went, they tried different places to see if the rod would sink. They walked many miles and travelled for a long time without success. One day they climbed a hill and saw a rainbow. Regarding it as a favorable omen, Manco Cápac tested the ground. At one thrust, the staff disappeared into the earth. So Manco Cápac and Mama Ocllo, his sister-wife, settled there and called the place Cuzco, the navel and center of the world. The Coricancha was erected over the very spot where Manco Cápac sank his golden rod."

"That legend is quite different from the one about the Ayar brothers," Mother remarked.

"It is," Father agreed. "They differ in some ways but agree in others and both say Manco Cápac and Mama Ocllo founded Cuzco. Keep in mind that the Torah has slightly different creation stories in Genesis One and Genesis Two. And the gospels of Matthew and Luke describe the birth of Jesus but vary the details, while Mark and John don't mention it at all."

"Maybe people just remember different things," Yaya suggested. "Or they focus on different things when they tell a story. That happens with my friends."

"That's a likely explanation," Father said. "But myths may also seem inconsistent because they tell of the extraordinary—things ordinary language cannot easily describe."

"Why bother telling them?" Yaya asked.

"They offer insights into the culture of those who believe the myth," Father replied. "The story of the golden rod explains the importance of the hill we're climbing. Ever since Manco

Cápac, there have been temples here. The Inca king Pachacuti replaced them with a grand complex that he called Inticancha, the sun's courtyard.

"We know it as the Coricancha," he continued. "Its temples crowned a series of agricultural terraces that descended to the Huatanay River, which in turn flowed into the Urubamba and eventually to the Amazon River.

"Coricancha means golden enclosure or golden courtyard. Before being vandalized by the Spanish, its temples had been filled inside and out with gold. One outside wall that faced southeast had been fully sheathed in gold," said Father. "Imagine the sight of that gilded temple wall virtually igniting as beams from the rising sun reached it each morning."

After the glowing image my imagination had conjured up, the Church of Santo Domingo was a disappointment. From the sidewalk, I only saw a big old stone church when we finally reached the site. Then Father pointed out the rows of Inca stonework along the street and the graceful, twenty-foot high curved wall at the end of the church.

The busy-ness of the immense baroque church overwhelmed the elegant Inca stonework. But due to an accident of fate, the calm Inca style was more evident inside. In 1950 a huge earthquake toppled the church. All it did to the Inca structures was crack a retaining wall. The Peruvian team that restored the buildings afterwards valued the Inca architecture more than the colonial, so a large section of the church cloister was not replaced and four Inca temples were left as freestanding structures within the reconstructed church.

Minus two large temples demolished by the Spanish—one for the father-sun god Inti, the other for the creator god Viracocha, what remains of the original Inca complex is a courtyard surrounded by four symmetrically arranged temples with walls of finely polished ashlars laid in neat, brick-like rows.

Though long gone, each temple had been adorned with murals and objects made of gold, silver, and precious gems. And their steeply pitched roofs had been covered with a log frame and an ichu grass thatch. When I asked why such elegant looking buildings would have such primitive roofs, Father explained that for centuries Peru—particularly Cuzco—has been in an active earthquake zone. A lightweight roof was safer.

One temple was dedicated to the Moon—Mama Quilla, the mother goddess who ruled marriage and the calendar. Another was for Thunder-Lightning—Chiqui Illapa, a fertility god linked to rain. A third was for the Rainbow—K'uychi, a fertility god linked to both rain and sun. The last was dedicated to the Stars, including Venus—Ch'asca Qoyllur or shaggy star, the goddess of maidens and flowers; the Southern Cross—Katachillay, the all-important guide-star; and the Pleiades—Qollqa, storehouse of abundant harvests and the mother of all the other stars.

Unlike Machu Picchu's wayronas, Coricancha's temples had walls on four sides and only one doorway. They had housed Inca mummies and important ritual objects including a huge solar disk and life-sized figures of animals and plants—all made of gold or silver. In a side courtyard there had even been a garden with realistic gold replicas of corn growing on the stalk.

"Pizarro demanded all the gold as ransom for the Inca king Atahualpa," Father added. "Once he got it, he killed the Inca, melted down the gold, and sent it all to Spain."

"That makes me sad," I told him. "Not because the gold is gone—the temples look beautiful as they are. I'm sorry the king got killed and that Pizarro's heart and mind were overtaken by such dark forces."

Mother hugged me as she whispered, "Me too." Yaya nodded in agreement.

Father regarded me tenderly and said, "My love, you are speaking the language of the heart."

As the Tahuantinsuyo's principal shrine, the Coricancha stood at the center of forty ceremonial paths called ceques, pilgrimage routes to shrines or haucas that radiated like spokes on a wheel in all directions. Pilgrims who traveled here seeking special blessings or a consultation with the oracle had to observe strict fasts and enter barefoot, carrying heavy burdens as a sign of humility.

A high priest presided over the complex and oversaw hundreds of priests. Priestesses were in charge of the Moon temple and supervised the many mamaconas or ñustas.

After viewing everything inside, we went out and walked along the terrace supported by the beautiful curved wall. It was the highest of a series of terraces. Several levels below was a large plaza where sacred corn, called Sara Mama—Corn Mother, had been raised by the ñustas for making ceremonial chicha.

While my parents were taking photos with Yaya, I went looking for my stone-friend. Before long I came across an open door on the side of the church. I was surprised to see the Elder from the Mountain standing there, beckoning me. As I approached, she slipped inside. I followed and she went behind the altar. She didn't come out again, so I went to see where she was.

On the floor between the altar and the sanctuary, was a hatch that opened onto steep stone steps. I was wondering what to do when I heard the Elder say, "Tanis, have no fear. Follow me."

I was still standing there when a draft gave me goose bumps. The Elder called me again so I descended the steep steps backwards, like going down a ladder. When I reached the ground, I turned around and the hatch closed abruptly, leaving me in total darkness.

Feeling trapped, I became suddenly anxious. What if this was a trick by the dark forces Don José warned us about? I thought of Ojito and wished he were with me. I'd have liked his guidance as well as his company—and his light would have been a real help.

My mind was beginning to grow wild with fear when my eyes adjusted to the dark. I could now see that I was in a small room with stone walls and directly across from me was a stone-framed doorway. The Elder called again, so I passed through the door and entered a long tunnel.

Its walls had a luminous, greenish hue that let me see fairly well—at least enough to see the walls. I couldn't actually see the ground, so I moved cautiously, walking toe-first to test the ground before me, and made slow progress.

Before long, the tunnel began sloping down, making it harder to use my toe-test method. Then I noticed symbols that looked like tocapus etched into the walls.

"Señora," I called, hoping the Elder would answer. The only reply was my voice echoing back. That reminded me of Q'enqo. Then I thought of the Chinkana—the place where one gets lost. I was afraid to lose contact with the Elder, so I began moving faster, almost running.

The ground leveled off and the tunnel opened into a natural cave with niches in its walls and a stone altar. It had two exits. I chose the left one and entered a passageway in which I began to have trouble breathing, so I made my way back to the cave and took the other tunnel.

Eventually that tunnel forked and I chose the right-hand way. I hadn't gone far when my foot slipped on a slick. A bit beyond that, I accidentally kicked a stone that landed with a splash in some water. I stopped moving. Judging by the sound, the water was far below me. I knew the splash was a sign but it took a few minutes to realize that the stone had just warned me and probably saved me from falling into a deep underground lake. I began to panic when I realized that if the stone hadn't been there and I hadn't kicked it, I could be drowning.

My heart raced, my breathing quickened, and I was overcome by a sense of dread. But in the midst of my panic, a small voice inside me warned that such heavy energies would only be a handicap. So I took slow, deep breaths with the intention of releasing my fears. Trying to do what Don José described, I exhaled my heavy, fearful energies and inhaled what I hoped were healing energies.

The process helped so I continued doing it. Once my heart had stopped racing, I said prayers of gratitude to the stone, my guardian angel, Don José, and whatever else was protecting me. Then I turned back, calmer but on high alert.

At the previous fork, I had the option of heading back to the Coricancha or taking the other tunnel. Standing there, it dawned on me that I was in the underworld, the land of the dead and the unborn. I had no idea why I was here—or how I'd get out. Then the Elder called and, trusting she would lead me out, I followed the sound of her voice and took the alternate route.

I made a few more wrong turns, but none were as bad as nearly falling into the watery deeps. I finally figured out that when I came to a fork, the greenish light increased in one direction and diminished in the other—and it was wiser to take the brighter fork.

Gradually, the texture of the ground changed. It went from hard and dry to a damp, mossy texture. Then it became an upward flight of stone steps. I saw light above me and emerged to find that I was in the Chinkana area of Sacsayhuamán.

Relieved to be outside again, it took a while for my eyes to adjust to the light. Then I spotted the old woman. She was forty feet away, beckoning. I quickened my pace and saw her go between two of Sacsayhuamán's huge stones. I followed.

After descending a long flight of steps, I entered a passage with many wall niches. The floor sloped down for a while and then leveled off. Suddenly I found myself in a huge cave with fine niches that reminded me of where I'd seen the Elder in my Machu Picchu vision. Hoping she would appear, I waited a few minutes. When she didn't, I knew I had to keep going.

Spotting some small stones on the ground, I picked them up in case I wanted a warning device and left by the only exit. The route out of the cave meandered and twisted in a way that made me think it had been created by running water.

I was getting used to travelling underground when the sound of wailing voices made me feel incredibly sad. Soon after, the tunnel opened into a huge cave filled by a lake. Although a narrow stone ledge had been carved along one side of it, I was afraid to continue. The water was well below the path and there seemed no way out of the lake. I wondered if the wailing voices were from people who had drowned there. I wondered if I would become one of them.

Just then I thought of Mother and wanted to turn around. She and Father were probably worried about me. I really wanted to see them and became so conflicted I didn't know what to do. So I did the only thing that made sense. I meditated.

I sat with my back to the wall and breathed slowly as I asked for guidance. Though it took a while, I got a sense that I was meant to take this journey. I said a prayer of gratitude for my new clarity and, before stepping onto the narrow ledge, I deposited three of the stones I had been carrying. One was for the fear I wanted to leave behind, one was a prayer for protection going forward, and one was a fervent wish that the lloronas—the wailing voices, would find solace.

Despite my resolve to stay calm, I didn't breathe easily until I reached the far side of the lake and entered another tunnel. That's when I recalled that Don José said the poq'pos in a family were connected. So while I trekked through what seemed like miles of interconnected passageways, I tried to draw strength from my family's poq'po. Whether it was that or something else, I felt that I was being protected.

After walking for hours, I tripped and fell forward. From my neck down I was on solid ground, but my knee hurt and my head hung over a chasm. I was looking straight into a fissure that went to the very center of the Earth. I gasped and skittered backwards.

As I lay sprawled on the ground, I noticed a quiet murmur and listened intently. It seemed to be a heartbeat that wasn't mine. Suddenly alert, I sat up and tried to figure out what it was coming from—and where. I immediately had visions of a huge puma lurking just out of sight. But once that fear had run through my mind, I realized the sound was curiously calming... and somehow familiar.

I turned my head in every direction and finally leaned over the chasm. The sound was coming from way down—from the crystal heart of the planet. So I pressed my back against a wall and breathed slowly. I can't say how long I did it but as I did, the quiet rhythm of the planet's heartbeat filled and calmed my own.

Before leaving, I put three stones near the wall. One was to thank my guardian angel for protecting me, one was a prayer that others on this path would avoid the perilous drop, and one was an offering to Pachamama: I was in her keeping and wanted to honor her as well as ask for her support.

That was the worst of it. I returned to the last fork I'd encountered and took the other route. Before long I saw the Elder moving rapidly ahead of me. The tunnel led me to a cave like the one where I first met her. Happily this one opened onto the floor of a lowland jungle.

I stepped outside and was inundated by hot humid air, the scent of flowers and damp earth, and a cacophony of birdcalls and monkey cries. The tree canopy was so dense that only shafts of sunlight filtered through. One shone directly on the Elder who stood facing me. Behind her were stone buildings overgrown with tropical vegetation. Despite the low ground, something about the place reminded me of Machu Picchu.

"Congratulations on both your resolve and your faith, Tanis!" the old woman said warmly. "Welcome to Paititi, the Heart of the Heart. This is the true hidden city of the Incas. It can only be reached by a treacherous jungle canyon, and only those who speak the language of the heart can enter here and return alive."

Trying to make sense of what she said, I asked why I hadn't seen a canyon.

"You came through the Ukju Pacha," she explained. "Challenged to integrate past-life wisdom with wisdom from this life, your underworld journey was an initiation."

"To what?"

"Being a messenger, my child. You are a wise old soul who knows the language of the heart. You were chosen to experience things on behalf of others so you could share what you learned." Then, sweeping her arm toward the buildings behind her, she added, "Many years ago, this holy place was closed off from the outside world until the day when humans had advanced spiritually and could successfully reach it—as you did. Now you are able to use what lies here."

"What is that, Señora?"

"Knowledge of the true history and purpose of life on Earth," she replied.

Beckoning me to follow, the Elder almost flew through streets thick with jungle growth until we came to an enormous hole that looked like a meteorite crater. In its center was a huge meteorite. Taking a zigzag path we went down one side of the crater and entered a vast subterranean room.

Once my eyes adjusted to the dimness, I noticed some large, pyramidal crystals. Each was bigger and wider than me. Beyond them was a stone altar full of elongated golden objects the Elder called a library. I went to examine them and saw that they were inscribed with cryptic shapes.

"Señora, how do you read the books?"

"We don't read them—we sing them," she replied.

I could read musical notes, but the shapes on the books mystified me, so I asked how.

"To sing this library you need a magical key in the form of a cosmic name—a unique musical phrase found deep within your heart and soul. Like a computer password, it lets you access essential information. It also activates psychic abilities."

"I don't even know if I have one," I said. "At least, I can't remember it."

"Each person has a cosmic name and no two are alike. Remembering your name is a gift that only occurs at the right moment," she explained.

"Who gives it?"

"A cosmic name can be given in various ways. You might receive one during meditation in answer to an internal question. It might come in a dream as a name that's repeated again and again. Or it might come as a revelation from your guides."

"What do you do with the name?" I asked.

"Chant it," she replied. "Your cosmic name awakens memories of previous lives and helps reveal future undertakings—both personal and collective. It is a vibratory key that can unlock important secrets, including this archive. Yet singing your cosmic name involves more than making sounds with your throat. You must actually raise your vibration. A cosmic name is like a tuning fork. First it vibrates within you, then it expands and elevates your resonance, then it projects your energy outward into the universe. But it's also like a spiritual antenna."

I was totally confused so I asked for an example.

"I cannot tell you another person's name, though perhaps I can explain it better," the Elder said. "A cosmic name identifies and acknowledges your purpose through the ages. It also indicates your kaypa—the context within which you must work to strengthen and balance yourself spiritually. Think of it as a unique mantra that you can use to reach higher spiritual planes and discover your mission in life. But truly, my child, the only way to understand this is by remembering your cosmic name."

"How can I do that, Señora?"

"Sit in a comfortable position. Get centered. Extend both arms forward from your shoulders with palms facing out. Close your eyes and become aware of your heartbeat. Take slow, deep breaths and allow your heart to speak to you," the Elder coached.

I did as she suggested. I sat in the lotus position, extended my arms, and listened.

"Open your mind and senses," she urged. "You should hear a whisper coming from your chest. You will recognize a sound that feels like the name of a dear friend."

After a while, she asked, "What do you hear?"

"I don't hear anything."

"Keep listening!" she admonished.

Eventually I heard what sounded like bells. I saw something in my mind's eye and heard a word. It sounded like Ez... Ez... Ezriah—or something like that. Although I had not yet uttered it aloud, the Elder said, "Excellent!"

"Ezriah, Ezriah, Ezriah, Ezriah..." I said aloud, happily repeating my name over and over.

"Getting your cosmic name is another major initiation, an acknowledgment that you have achieved an expanded consciousness," she said. "Beyond that, it serves as the key to your inner self. Nonetheless, the key is neither the door nor the hand that turns the key. While it is well and good to have such a key, you must also know how to use it."

"How do I use it?"

"Chant your cosmic name aloud—especially in the morning. Like the magic phrase *open sesame*, chanting opens interior pathways and sharpens extrasensory perceptions. If you maintain a positive attitude and chant in a spirit of love and kindness, it fosters spiritual equilibrium and lets you find your authentic self. To achieve full spiritual awakening, each of us must remember, chant, and use our cosmic name.

"We condition our bodies by exercising and taking in proper nourishment," she continued. "We condition ourselves spiritually by meditating. Making it a habit strengthens us internally for situations when clarity and awareness are needed. It also fosters spiritual, mental, and physical health. So start chanting your name."

I sang my cosmic name and, as I did, a pleasant aroma filled the room—an aroma that seemed to come from me. Then the huge crystals began vibrating and glowing, giving the room a radiant light. There seemed to be an acoustic connection between the crystals and the golden books, a form of musical harmony that made my heart vibrate. Or was my heart making everything else vibrate? I couldn't tell.

I continued singing and began seeing images. I watched flashes of faces and places, often with a sense of déjà vu. I felt connected to a vast flowing—an immense awareness, an oceanic knowing. I took in the Akashic records of the history of humanity and the cosmos. Then I was immersed in a stream of consciousness that grew into wisdom teachings.

I felt myself transforming within a space-time spiral that surpassed the reach of three-dimensionality. All sensory and extrasensory perceptions integrated with a cosmic vastness. Expanded beyond myself I became one with the universe.

My body had no boundaries.

I was essentially limitless…

At some point, a state of completeness was reached. Then a vaguely disorienting process of reintegration began. My body tried to take in my newly expanded essence and I felt the limits of my previous sense of self. Having realized the fullness of who I am, my three-dimensional body and everyday mind seemed so confining.

I stopped singing and sat in silence for quite a while, content to simply be. But reentering was bittersweet. I simultaneously felt a sense of fullness—like there was nothing missing—and a sense of loss.

Eventually, the Elder asked how I felt.

"Different," I replied. "Spacious and incredibly peaceful."

"Would you help me do something of great consequence?" she inquired.

I said yes and we entered a complex of buildings that reminded me of the Coricancha. Within the largest temple was an immense golden disk with a human face and cat's eyes. It was surrounded by a halo of twelve rings. Although seemingly made of gold, the disk was semi-translucent—like a thinly silvered mirror.

"This is the thirteenth disk," said the Elder. "Are you willing to help open a portal through which the Earth can pass into the era of prophecy?"

"Is this the disk that unites the others?" I asked.

"Yes, my child, it is."

I sensed that Ojito had been preparing me for this for a long time—as had my experiences here and in the magical valley. And so, feeling both honored and a bit nervous, I replied, "I am at your service, Señora."

She told me to sit before the disk and extend my arms, palms out, while chanting my cosmic name. As I did, the disk spun on an unseen axis and the temple transformed. An image of the room that housed the golden library and pyramidal crystals flickered in and out of sight, alternately superimposed over the temple. At certain moments, both seemed to coexist in the same time-space.

"The disk has been activated!" the Elder cried exultantly. "We, the ancestors, are grateful for your help. In different parts of the world, other enlightened people working with helpful Piscorunas are activating the remaining disks. Soon, all thirteen will be aligned so they can open the portal that will let the great time shift happen."

I just sat gazing into the disk and listening to the jungle's sounds. I sat for a considerable length of time in a dream-like state. Then I seemed to wake up and suddenly felt tired.

"Señora, I've been away from my parents for too long. I should return."

"And so you shall, Tanis," the Elder assured me. "You will return before you have left."

As she said that I recalled how I had once passed through a light portal that transported me to Ganymede. Because I was journeying in real time, the seemingly long duration of my space travel did not correspond to the seconds of Earth-time I was gone.

When I turned my attention back to the Elder, she was saying, "You will return through the dimensional portal you just opened. Come closer to the disk."

Following her directions, I touched the disk's surface. My hand passed through as if it were a holographic image. Then a powerful force pulled me and I found myself back at the church doorway, just about to enter. At that moment, Mother called so I turned around.

"Don't stray too far," she said. "We're about to leave."

Together we exited to the street. While my parents checked out some postcards being offered by an enthusiastic vendor, Yaya and I went to see some Inca stones in the wall along the sidewalk. The beautiful greenish stones bent around a corner of the Coricancha's exterior.

Just then a female voice said, "Hola, Tanis."

Still a bit spacey from all I'd been through, I asked, "Who's speaking?"

"Not me," Yaya replied as she walked away to see something else.

With no clue who was speaking or where she was, I asked, "Where are you?"

"In the wall," she answered—and then my mental light went on. I looked and there was my stone-friend, part of the majestic Coricancha.

"Oh stone-friend, I'm so glad to see you," I cried. "I looked and looked for you."

I put my hands on the wall and touched my forehead and fingers to the stone. She had prepared my mind and heart for what I learned on my journey through the Sacred Valley, so I thanked her and sent images from everywhere. I was just finishing with Paititi when mother called to say it was time to return to the hotel.

"I must go," I said. "But now that I know where you are, I'll return in my dreams."

"Until then," the stone responded.

*Tanis finds Ojito at the Coricancha stone wall*

# 16

## *Epilogue*

I've returned to the Sacred Valley several times, yet that first visit remains the most magical and the experiences I had then are still unfolding.

"As above, so below—as within, so without" is the essence of what I learned from the highlanders who know everything is connected. Being wise observers of the world within and around them, they can experience multiple realities at the same time. They can also radiate harmony from the inside out. But trying to manifest "as within, so without" is not always easy for me. Through practice and discipline, however, staying composed and hopeful sustains me in situations that otherwise might overwhelm me.

Though not materially rich, the highlanders have something truly priceless: a world where the land and the people are in balance. Their love for Pachamama and all living things—water, stones, and stars included—shows this. It's also evident in the mutual give-and-take they call ayni and their devotion to the communal good. The old woman with the firewood who I met in Chinchero didn't complain about her burden, nor was she unhappy about it. Now I see her as a magician who co-created her own reality: by choosing to find the good in her situation, she transformed it. So when I feel like complaining, it helps to remember her. Sometimes I even hear her saying, "The less you think about a burden, the less it weighs you down."

In Paititi, I connected with the essence of Self beyond myself and felt the indescribable joy of being *in contact*. The routines and distractions of my everyday world make it easy to forget that I'm always connected—until something unexpected triggers a rift in space-time and I find myself smiling as I remember…

I try to sustain that sense of contact with the help of dreams, meditation, and my guides. Though I seldom talk about them now, I am blessed by and grateful for the continued presence of Ojito and the Elder from the Mountain in my life as spiritual guides.

When I can transcend the limits of my rationally conditioned mind, reality expands. In that magical realm stones can speak. Merged in an Inca wall, they sing the music of the cosmos. It's easy to miss that if one thinks of stones and temples as lifeless, but those who listen with an open heart can hear it. Each gets a different message, though, because each brings a unique gift to the world and each must take a unique path through it.

As a child I heard the beat of the planet's crystal heart on my journey through the underworld. But even in ordinary situations, children have the advantage of attending to things that adults take for granted. Until it is brainwashed away, children know that everything is alive, everything has feelings, and everything speaks to those who listen.

We all must listen carefully now because Pachamama is undergoing what the Q'ero describe as a pachacuti—an era of confusion and world-changing events. When the transition ends, a new and better era may emerge. However it won't happen overnight and it can't happen unless people are attentive and caring and willing to find remedies for Earth's problems. Activating the golden disk in Paititi was part of a process of change that I sustain in my everyday life by being heart-centered, guarding against the dark forces within me, and practicing ayni by doing what I can for my community and the world.

Pachacuti aside, life is essentially change. So when unforeseen events or difficulties knock me off balance, I try to see what they have to offer. Even problems may bring gifts. At the very least, they are opportunities to make conscious choices. Sometimes I must change—sometimes the situation must change. If I can find the teachings that come with change, I have the option to grow and self-transform.

Of all the amazing things that happened on my first journey through the magical valley, the gift of my cosmic name was the most profound because it put everything else into perspective. My parents called me Tanis, a name that means initiation. The life mission it seeded was meant to awaken Ezriah, the helper.

The first time I uttered Ezriah, my heart leapt at the sound—and still does. That name acknowledges my life purpose! And to this day, I do as the Elder from the Mountain advised: I chant my cosmic name each morning.

Chanting Ez-ri-ah fills me. It fills my bedroom, the house, and beyond. As I chant, I hear Ezriah chanting back—a melodious voice from beyond that recognizes me as we become one through the ages. From there, the world around me expands. From there, life manifests abundance and regeneration. From there, I know that love is who I've always been. From there, my ancestors and my ancestors' ancestors—all the way to their star ancestors—live through me.

In contact, I am Ezriah. The Helpful One.

# Glossary

*Non-English words below are in Quechua.*

**Apu** — Spirit guardian of the mountain. Considered the most powerful nature spirit, Apus contains an energizing or vitalizing force often linked to water. See also **Ñusta**.

**Ashlar** — A large, well-worked stone used to form a wall. For the Inca, stone had an essence or kamay that was independent of its form. Stone was also sacred and its sanctity was embedded in its material—not its form. Thus, the stones in a temple wall were as sacred as the temple contents. See also **Kamay**.

**Astral Journey** — During sleep or a shamanic trance, a person's spirit body, a double of her/his physical body, travels and has experiences as s/he dreams. The astral body is a vehicle for hopes and emotions.

**Ayar Brothers** — Mythical founders of the Inca dynasty. One version of their legend refers to eight siblings. Along with their four sister-wives, four brothers were sent by their heavenly father Inti to help the people of Earth. After traveling underground, the four brothers and four sisters emerged from the middle of three caves on a hillside and went in search of good land for farming. Three brothers—Ayar Cachi, Ayar Uchu, and Ayar Auca—were transformed into holy stones or huacas. The last brother, Ayar Manco, reached what is now Cuzco where he found good farmland. He changed his name to Manco Cápac, built a city there, established a code of laws, and taught people how to grow maize. With his sister-wife Mama Ocllo, he ruled for many years.

**Ayni** — Reciprocity; mutual give-and-take. The key Andean principle of human interaction, ayni sets up a sustainable balance between getting and giving. Voluntarily giving back.

**Chakana** — A three-stepped, Andean cross that represents a bridge between worlds; each step of the cross embodies one of the three worlds in Inca cosmology. The symbol for Katachillay or Southern Cross constellation, the "guide-star" of the southern hemisphere because it is clearly visible year-round. See also **Hanan Pacha; Kay Pacha; Ukju Pacha.**

**Contact** — A deep state of inner balance and harmony; a profound connection to the Self beyond the self. Also a physical encounter with an extraterrestrial or its vehicle.

**Cosmic Name** — A vibrational name-sound that emerges in the course of spiritual growth to identify and acknowledge a person's purpose through the ages. The cosmic name awakens memories of previous existences and helps reveal future undertakings, both personal and collective. To function, it must be sung or chanted in a way that raises the singer's vibration. Like a tuning fork, the name-sound first vibrates within the singer, then expands and elevates the singer's resonance, and finally projects the singer's energy outward into the universe.

**Experimenters** — A group of extraterrestrials that traveled backwards through space-time by means of dimensional portals to prevent Earth's total destruction. They created an alternate Earth-time that was incompatible with the real time of the universe, the fourth dimension.

**Extraterrestrial** — An intelligent being or life form that originated somewhere other than Earth, often abbreviated as ET. See also **Piscorunas.**

**Fourth Dimension** — The real time of the universe or the space-time continuum. In modern physics, space and time are combined in a four-dimensional field called space-time.

**Hanan Pacha** — The upper world or heavens, one of three worlds in the Andean cosmology. It is symbolized by the condor. See also **Kay Pacha; Ukju Pacha.**

**Highlanders** — The indigenous people of the high Andes. See also **Quechua; Runa.**

**Huaca** — Holy place of power, sacred site or shrine. Also the sacred energy of places in the landscape—including mountains, trees, springs, lakes or odd-shaped stones.

**Hucha** — A heavy, chaotic energy humans produce as a result of fear, grief, anxiety, guilt, anger, and unresolved conflicts. Hucha contaminates the body-heart-mind, causing illness and giving rise to dark forces. It is the opposite of sami. See also **Sami.**

**Inkarri** — A phonetic Quechua version of Inca Rey (Spanish for Inca King), Inkarri refers to the last Inca ruler. Different versions of the Inkarri legend involve one of three different men: Atahualpa who was killed by Pizzaro in 1533; Túpac Amaru who ruled a rebel state from Vilcabamba and was killed by colonial authorities in 1572; and the rebel Túpac Amaru II who was killed in 1781. In all accounts Inkarri vowed to avenge his death and the mistreatment of Peru's people, so his head was buried apart from his body. Legend says that when his head and body grow together again, Inkarri will rise and bring the end of times—an end to the disorder and darkness initiated by the Spanish—and allow the Andean people to reclaim their heritage. See also **End of Times**.

**Kamay** — Essence or the creative and enlivening force. The visible form of spiritual power.

**Kaypa** — A person's particular task; to make an effort.

**Kay Pacha** — The everyday or Earthly world, the middle of three worlds in Andean cosmology. It is symbolized by the puma. See also **Hanan Pacha; Ukju Pacha.**

**Manco Cápac** — The legendary first Inca king. The eldest Ayar brother who, along with his sister-wife Mama Ocllo, founded Cuzco and the Inca lineage. See also **Ayar Brothers**.

**Ñusta** — In Inca society, a ñusta was the princess-daughter of an Inca king. Ñustas were also the young women who lived as cloistered nuns in service to the divine sun. In the natural world, Ñustas are female water spirits that complement the mostly male Apus or mountain spirits. See also **Apu.**

**Pachacuti** — Earth-shaking; earthquake; disruption; violent tearing or breaking apart; world-changing.

The historic Inca king Pachacuti (1438-1471) took the name to define his role: he seized the right to rule, destroyed his enemies, and subdued neighboring tribes to expand the Inca Empire. The Spanish invasion (1532) was likewise a pachacuti—a disastrous, world-altering event for the Incas.

Andeans view time as cyclical so a pachacuti is a turning point in history, a world-reversing era, a period of turmoil and chaos followed by a harmonious transformation. The Q'ero and other Quechua believe the Earth is currently undergoing such a disruptive, world-changing period.

See also **Prophecies Regarding 2012; Q'ero.**

**Pachamama** — Mother Earth; the fruitful cosmic mother.

**Paititi** — The unconquered heart and soul of the Inca. The legendary ruins of a secret and sacred Inca city on the Upper Madre de Dios River in the Peruvian section of the Amazon rainforest. The archive of wisdom teachings hidden there is known as *The Book of the Ones Robed in White.*

**Piscorunas** — Bird-people or humanoid creatures with bird-like aspects. Beings from another plane, such as extraterrestrials, that act as go-betweens or messengers. Ancient deities with a mix of avian, feline, and human features as well as shamans who could fly to other worlds were also called Piscorunas. In colonial documents of Inca myths, references to birds or bird-shamans may be mythic codes for stars.

**Poq'po** — The luminous body or aura. A cocoon-like energy shield that surrounds and protects a person.

**Prophecies Regarding 2012** — Three Native American cultures see the year 2012 C.E. as a turning point. For the Maya it marks the end of the fifth cycle or time of darkness. For the Aztec it marks the beginning of the sixth sun. For the heirs of the Inca, the year marks the end of a pachacuti and the start of an era of positive spiritual transformation. In some prophecies, the December 2012 solstice is significant.

See also **Pachacuti; Q'ero.**

**Q'ero** — The Community of the Sanctuary. A remote group of Quechua-speaking people from the Peruvian Andes, the Q'ero are the spiritual and mystical keepers of ancient highland traditions. Many are paq'os or healers—what outsiders call shamans.

Q'ero villages are located in the mountains at elevations above 14,000 feet. The people are farmers and magnificent weavers who claim to be the last descendants of the Inca. According to their oral history their ancestors resisted the Spanish with the aid of the Apus. The Q'ero have long preserved the prophecy of a pachacuti as a result of which the current upside-down world will be put right and Inkarri will return.

See also **Apu; End of Times; Inkarri; Pachacuti**.

**Quechua** — The name for an indigenous people from the central Andes, especially in Peru, but also in Ecuador and Bolivia. Quechua is also the name for their language and its related dialects.

See also **Runa; Runasimi**.

**RAMA** — Alternately called Rama Mission or Misión Rahma, this global organization was founded by Sixto Paz Wells and others to educate the public about UFOs and ETs and to advance human spiritual growth. Derived from a reverse spelling of amar (Spanish for love), RAMA teachings hold that love is the most transformative force in the universe. Its teachings also hold that extraterrestrial contacts provide important messages but humans must determine how to apply them. For further information go to the website www.RahmaUnitedStates.com.

**Runa** — The people. What the Quechua people call themselves.

**Runasimi** — People-speak or people's speech, meaning the Quechua language.

**Sami** — Refined, consistent energy. The clean and healthy energy of the natural world. Sami is the light energy of healing that is transmitted through the energetic body or poq'po. It is the opposite of hucha.

See also **Hucha; Poq'po**.

**Times, End of** — Andean prophecies related to 2012 C.E. predict an end of times—not an end of time or the end of the world. For the Inca, time is cyclical, like the seasons, and spiral-shaped: when one era ends, another begins. Thus the end of times marks the birth of a new era that will merge the alternative Earth-time created by extraterrestrials with the real time of the universe, the fourth dimension.

See also **Prophecies Regarding 2012.**

**Ukju Pacha** — The underworld or inner world, one of three worlds in Andean cosmology. It is symbolized by the serpent. See also **Hanan Pacha; Kay Pacha.**

**Yanantin** — A concept central to the Andean worldview, yanantin implies masintin. The term refers to a dualistic yet balanced marriage of two distinct yet complementary equals. It represents the harmonious relationship between what "Western culture" usually sees as opposites—male and female, light and dark, right and left. Yanantin-masintin are complements similar to that of the Chinese yin-yang.

**Yanca** — Astronomer.